# LORD SAWSBURY SEEKS A BRIDE

If he is to protect his estate and save his sister from penury, Lord Simon Sawsbury must marry an heiress. Annabel Burgoyne has no desire to marry, but wishes to please her parents, who are offering a magnificent dowry in the hope of enticing an impecunious aristocrat. As Simon and Bella, along with their families, move to their Grosvenor Square residences for the Season, it's not long before the neighbours are drawn together. But when events go from bad to worse, will Simon sacrifice his reputation to marry Bella?

FENELLA J. MILLER

# LORD SAWSBURY SEEKS A BRIDE

*Complete and Unabridged*

**LINFORD**
*Leicester*

First published in Great Britain in 2019


First Linford Edition
published 2020

A catalogue record for this book is available
from the British Library.


ISBN 978–1–4448–4486–3


Published by
Ulverscroft Limited
Anstey, Leicestershire

Set by Words & Graphics Ltd.
Anstey, Leicestershire
Printed and bound in Great Britain by
T. J. International Ltd., Padstow, Cornwall

This book is printed on acid-free paper

# 1

Suffolk, February 1814.

'My lord, you have no other option. Unless you marry money, your estate will be forfeit and your brother and sister destitute.'

Simon was tempted to throw the nearest book at his lawyer but restrained the impulse. 'Foster, is there nothing else I can sell?'

'No, sir, there is not. Your father borrowed heavily against the estate and his debts must be paid by the summer.'

'Then I have no recourse but to open the house in Grosvenor Square and set things in motion. Emily can have her come-out ball at the same time.'

His lawyer was about to protest at this suggestion but Simon raised his hand. 'This is the last chance she might have to find herself a husband before we lose everything. I thank God that Richard is safe at school and knows nothing of this disaster.'

'On consideration, my lord, I think your suggestion to be sensible. There is more chance of you acquiring yourself an heiress if you do not look too desperate. At least your estates are in good heart and have been managed well despite the depredations that your father made to fund his gambling.'

'I shall need to borrow more in order to bring this off, Foster. Can you obtain the wherewithal to fund this final throw of the dice?'

'I can, my lord. The bank would prefer you to pay your debts rather than take your estate from you. However, Lady Emily will not be able to purchase a new wardrobe but will have to manage with what she has. I think it unlikely there will be more than just enough to open the house and hold a ball.'

Simon surged to his feet, indicating the meeting was over. He rang the bell placed on the side of his desk and the waiting footman appeared, ready to escort his lawyer out.

It was a damnable business and he blamed himself for not realising sooner that his father had gambled away the family fortune. He suspected now that the accident with the pistol had been suicide. No point in repining over what was done; he must now do everything he could to rectify matters.

He was about to go in search of his sister when she burst into the study. 'What did he say? Is it as bad as you feared?'

'It is, Emily, and we must both parade in London this Season in order to find ourselves a rich partner.'

She seemed unbothered by his comment. 'Then it's fortunate I can design my own gowns and that Molly and I can sew them. All I need is the latest fashion plates and I can assure you I will be in the first stare of fashion.'

'Gentlemen's attire does not change

so rapidly so I've no need to replace anything of mine. I take it there's still a plentiful supply of the Indian materials our grandfather brought back with him?'

'There is indeed. If we are to hold a ball in my honour then we must set a date and send out invitations in the next week or two. The beginning of May is the best time as the weather won't be too hot and our guests won't yet be jaded from attending too many routs, soirées and balls.'

'Then I'll leave those arrangements in your capable hands, sweetheart, and go to Town and see what needs doing at the house. I thought we could transfer the staff from here and not employ fresh for our stay in London.'

She took his place at the desk and was busy scribbling down the families they must invite to the ball. Emily was six years his junior and at nineteen might be considered a little old to be a debutante. However, the fact that they had been in mourning for a year was explanation enough for her late arrival on the marriage mart.

His sister was above average height, slender and shared the same colouring as him. Her eyes were a dark blue and her hair a rich, nut-brown. She had fashionable ringlets and he was certain with her wit and beauty she would have no difficulty finding herself a suitable husband.

She glanced up and smiled. 'Do I pass muster, brother? Brunettes are not *de rigeur* this year but I hope my impeccable pedigree will compensate for that.'

'I am the Earl of Sawsbury. That will have to be sufficient as I have nothing else to offer.'

She laughed. 'Good heavens, brother, have you looked in the glass recently? You're a veritable Adonis; young ladies will be swooning at your feet. The only reason you've not been snapped up before now is because you've avoided London during the Season.'

'I've not been *snapped up* as you so

politely put it because matrimony does not interest me. Having watched our parents destroy each other, and our grandparents before that, I've been in no hurry to put my head in parson's mousetrap.'

'Both our grandparents and parents married for love and we intend to do so for pragmatic reasons. Neither of us believe in romantic love — we know that doesn't last. However, I'm certain a business arrangement will work splendidly for both of us.' She held up her hand and counted on her fingers. 'These are the things that we need to find in the one we choose: one, respect; two, liking; three, intelligence; four, a sense of humour. If whoever we choose has these attributes I'm certain we will be content.'

There was something else he wanted but he could hardly add this to her list. Mentioning physical desire to his younger sister would not be appropriate.

'There's one essential you neglected

to mention: whoever we choose must have deep pockets. Another thing is that I don't think we both need to make this sacrifice. Shall we agree that if one of us meets someone who fits our list of requirements the other can then withdraw?'

'Absolutely not. I wish to be married and have children of my own to love — and it's high time you set up your own nursery.' She tapped the paper in front of her. 'Go away, Simon, and leave me to compile my list. You have to go to Town immediately and discover what dates have already been taken. It would be an absolute disaster to hold our ball on the same day as someone else. Another thing: we shall require tickets for Almack's.'

He was unable to prevent his look of horror at the thought of attending such a dismal place. Her laughter followed him out. Fortunately, it was no more than a few hours' journey to Town and if he set off at first light tomorrow he could be there before dark.

★  ★  ★

'Miss Annabel Burgoyne, if you don't come down from the tree this instant I shall insist that your father takes a birch to you when you do descend.'

Bella smiled at her irate mama. 'We both know he'll do no such thing. Anyway, Papa has never raised a hand to me and is unlikely to do so now that I'm full-grown.'

Her mother put her hands on her hips and glared up into the bare branches of the massive oak tree. 'Why must you be so perverse? I cannot think of another young lady who has just been told they are to have a London Season, that their papa has taken a house in the most prestigious part of Town, that they are to have an entirely new wardrobe and . . . '

'Mama, all that would be delightful if I didn't know you expected me to choose an aristocratic husband by the end of it.' With a sigh of resignation, she dropped to the lower branches and then swung to the ground. If she'd been wearing a gown and not men's breeches this would have been impossible.

'Here I am. I apologise for upsetting you. I know that you and Papa wish for me to marry well and I give you my word I'll do my best. Have you considered that although I'm considered beautiful and am most likely the young lady with the biggest dowry, these things might not compensate for my ancestry.'

'I know, I know, my love. Being the daughter of a gentleman who made his fortune in trade, and whose grandfather was a groom, is not something to be proud of . . . '

'Enough of that, Mama. I refuse to be ashamed that I have not a drop of aristocratic blood in my body. There are bound to be impoverished aristocrats desperate to marry an heiress, even one like me, and I shall do my best to entice one of them to offer for me.'

Her mother's anger melted like snow in the sunshine and she was embraced.

'We shall leave the choice to you as you have a sensible head on your shoulders. There's no rush; you're only nineteen years of age, you can have two further Seasons before you will be considered on the shelf. Your father and I have no wish for you to marry anyone you cannot like.'

'I've no intention of doing so. I'm not sure what I want in a husband but I'm absolutely certain what I don't want. I shall not look in the direction of a dissolute gentleman, a gambler, a drinker or a violent man. He must be kind, personable and reasonably intelligent — apart from that I've no preferences.'

'Will you not be curious as to why he might be impecunious?'

'I'm assuming that his father will have ruined the family finances and the son is now doing what he can to put matters right.'

Her father was waiting inside to speak to her. 'Bella, I have here a list of possible candidates. I've had them vetted so you can be assured they're not vicious in any way.' He handed her two sheets of closely written paper.

'Good heavens! I'd no idea there would be so many for me to choose from. I'm going to change and will then peruse this with interest. I won't ask how your man obtained this information.'

Her maid, Annie, had hot water and clean clothes awaiting her arrival. It took less than half an hour to restore her appearance from disgraceful to acceptable. She viewed herself in the long glass and nodded.

Chestnut hair and vivid green eyes were not to everybody's taste, but they made her stand out in a crowd. Her features were regular, she had curves in all the expected places and a perfect set of teeth. She was sanguine that if her beloved papa managed to obtain vouchers for Almack's assembly rooms she would turn a few heads.

Fortunately, he had a couple of prestigious connections, members of the *ton* that he had lent money to at an advantageous rate; both gentlemen had promised to get her name on the list and also have them included in all the important invitations. From then on it would be up to her to find herself a husband she could be happy with.

'I don't remember wearing this gown before, Annie.'

'You have so many, miss, I doubt that you'll ever wear them all. Pale green velvet is perfect with your colouring.'

She supposed that if she spent more time correctly dressed and less time raking around the place in men's clothing, riding astride, behaving as if she was the son of the house and not a daughter, more of her extensive wardrobe would be worn.

With the list in her hand she headed for her sitting room and curled up on the window seat, where one found the best light. February could be unpleasant but the weather had been remarkably clement and the weak, winter sunshine was sufficient for her to be able to read the interesting information on the sheets of paper.

As she read she understood that

another requirement for her future husband was his age. She scrambled from her perch and sat at her desk. Picking up a pen, she trimmed it, uncorked the ink and was ready to slash a line through those over thirty-five. Sixteen years older than her was more than enough.

This left a dozen and she decided to remove widowers as well. She had no wish to be mama to someone else's children — the only reason she'd agreed to marry was because she wanted babies of her own.

Papa had not thought to include any physical description of the gentlemen, just their ages, locations and their reasons for being available to a hopeful debutante. There were now only seven to consider, which would make things easier.

Her smile was rueful as she read the pages again. No doubt these aristocratic would-be bridegrooms were also studying a similar list with the names of heiresses on it. She rather thought she would come at the bottom of the list because of her family — any of them would prefer a young lady who was gently born.

Although they were to reside in Grosvenor Square — the largest square in London, where all the houses were of modern construction and quite splendid — there was little point in arranging a ball for herself as no one of importance would accept their invitations. They must rely on smaller events, card parties, musical evenings, that sort of thing.

Her parents were, as always, sitting together in the study. In the winter they rarely bothered to use the main reception rooms as they were too difficult to heat. They held no parties and received few invitations, so what was the point in wasting fuel?

'Well, what do you think of the selection I've found for you?'

'Papa, I removed those I'm not interested in and this leaves just seven possible gentlemen. How do you intend to ensure that I meet them all?' Not waiting for an answer, she continued with the concern that was uppermost in her mind. 'I think the most eligible of these bachelors might well not be available to me as they will naturally select a young lady who not only has money but also a reasonable pedigree. I expect there are several of those . . . '

'Annabel, if the girl has money and breeding then she won't be looking at these gentlemen. She will have the pick of the crop. Rest assured, you will be competing with girls from a similar background to yours and I doubt that any of them can compare to you.'

She dropped into the nearest chair feeling foolish. 'Of course. I really have not thought this through. Those you have on your list will be more desperate to find themselves a wife they can bear to live with than I am to find myself an aristocratic husband. Our wealth comes from shipping and other manufactories but I defy anyone to discern any difference in my behaviour, education or manners to the daughter of a duke.'

Mama nodded vigorously. 'Indeed, my love, you are right to say so. We spared no expense on your upbringing, you had the best tutors and governesses money could buy. Your papa and I have done our best to improve our own diction and I think we would pass muster in any drawing room.'

She hated the fact that they had felt obliged to change in order to be accepted by members of a Society who she thoroughly despised. The ladies led a life of idleness, were waited on hand and foot and the gentlemen were no better. The thought of marrying into the *ton* and being obliged to behave as if she didn't have a sensible thought in her head filled her with dismay.

'I've come to a decision, and I fear it might be one you disapprove of. However much you wish me to marry an aristocrat, I'll not do so unless he accepts you as you are. He must be prepared to welcome you into his family and introduce you to all his friends without hesitation.'

They exchanged a worried glance. Her father cleared his throat. 'Then I fear the venture is doomed to fail. I cannot imagine there's an aristocrat in the country who would welcome us into their house. No, we are resigned to seeing very little of you or our future grandchildren. Our aim is for you to join the aristocracy.'

She looked from one to the other in shock. 'That's fustian. I'll not marry anyone who wishes to shun you. You are my beloved parents and you will always be part of my life and that of any children I might be blessed with, and that's an end to the matter.'

'Darling child, you're well aware that we're somewhat older than most parents with a girl your age. There was no time for children any earlier as we were too busy building up the business. Your papa was travelling abroad with his ships whilst I ran the offices here. It's our dearest wish to see you well settled before we go to meet our maker . . . '

'Neither of you have reached your

sixtieth year; you're fit and healthy. I'm certain you will both live to be octogenarians, so I'll hear no more of that nonsense.'

'Then are we to proceed with this venture or do you wish us to cancel the arrangements?' Her father waited for her answer.

'No, we shall continue. I've made my feelings clear and as long as you don't have unrealistic expectations then the whole thing might be quite enjoyable. Something has occurred to me, Mama. If you're so certain you'll not be welcomed into the best drawing rooms or receive invitations to the prestigious parties, who is then to accompany me? I can hardly go on my own.'

'We have employed the relic of one Sir Humphrey Jones. She has impeccable breeding but he left her all but destitute. She will be joining us here next week and will oversee the arrangements from then on. I have been reliably informed she is received everywhere.'

Papa smiled benevolently at Mama's

comment. 'I intend to provide her with a new wardrobe and sufficient funds to be able to live comfortably for several years — I shall buy her a small estate if she is successful in finding you an aristocrat that you are prepared to marry.'

# 2

Simon left Sawsbury Hall at dawn. His valet, Mason, thundered along behind him with his overnight baggage. Their horses were massive, and well up to the task of carrying them all the way to Town as long as they were given time to rest on the journey.

His trunk was following behind in a closed carriage, along with a skeleton staff, who would be able to cater for his needs at the house in Grosvenor Square. He stopped for refreshments and to give the horses a well-earned breather at the Red Lion in Colchester.

This town was bustling — it was market day and the main thoroughfare was redolent of cattle and other farm beasts, so he decided not to venture from the inn. Two hours later he set off again and arrived in Chelmsford, where he allowed the horses to recuperate for a second time at the Saracens Head. Eventually, he reached his overnight destination in Romford and was glad to wash the grime of the long ride from his person and devour a substantial supper.

'Mason, bring me my shaving water at dawn. I want to be in London by midday.'

'Yes, my lord. I fear it's going to be raining tomorrow. The skies are black and there's thunder around.'

'Then we shall get wet.'

He dismissed his man, who had accommodation somewhere in the attics, and fell into bed to be roused the following morning with the welcome smell of strong, dark coffee. This was his favourite beverage — he much preferred it to the insipid taste of tea that ladies appeared to enjoy.

The area of London he was obliged to travel through in order to reach his home was where the docks were. He had not travelled extensively and rather envied those men who made their living from the sea. Seeing the tall masts of the ships above the roofs of the houses reminded him of his grandfather, who had visited India in his youth and had brought back not only exotic materials and objects, but also a lovely young bride. They had met on board. Her father had been a director of the East India Company and was recently deceased — his widow and daughter were returning to England.

His grandpapa had yet to inherit the earldom, indeed had had an older brother in line before him, so married Isabel as soon as they docked in London without bothering to inform his parents. From all accounts they had been happy enough until his older brother broke his neck hunting and shortly afterwards the earl kicked the bucket.

The marriage had deteriorated from that moment. The countess produced three daughters before the required heir arrived and, if family gossip was to be believed, the marriage became in name only: his grandfather found solace in the arms of a series of mistresses.

His own papa, the solitary son, had grown up scarcely knowing his father and had then made the same mistake himself by marrying for love and not practical reasons. Simon shuddered as he recalled the screaming rows followed by weeks of arctic silence. When his mother had died in childbed producing his brother Richard, his father had been inconsolable and had taken to gambling and drink.

He had done his best to protect his siblings but he had been little more than a boy himself. On reaching his majority he had moved himself and the children to his own estate and they had not returned to Sawsbury Hall until the demise of their parent in a so-called hunting accident last year.

Romantic love was for fools. Marriage should be treated like any other business arrangement and by so doing those involved would avoid the appalling scenes and the emotional upheaval that his parents and grandparents had endured.

He dismounted at the rear of his house and handed the reins to his valet, who also acted as his groom when needed.

'Take care of the horses first. Although the windows are shuttered there's smoke coming from several chimneys so the caretakers are doing their job.'

His arrival was not noticed so he was obliged to hammer on the side door to gain entrance. Eventually the door was unbolted. A surprisingly young man bowed.

'Good day to you, my lord. Were we expecting you to come today? I fear the house isn't ready.'

'I only decided yesterday to come.' He stepped around the man, bracing himself to see decay and dirt. It had been several years since the house had been occupied during the Season. On the rare occasion he had needed to come to Town on business, he had stayed at The Clarendon Hotel in Bond Street.

To his surprise, the place was immaculate. There were fires lit — albeit meagre ones — in all the main reception rooms and the place was unexpectedly warm.

'How is this possible? I thought only you and your wife were here to take care of things.'

'I have three daughters and two sons old enough to earn their keep, my lord, and together we've kept your house in good order.'

Simon clapped the man on his shoulder. 'Whatever the family have been paying you, it's not enough.'

'We ain't paid a wage, my lord; we live here and eat well at your expense.'

Without hesitation Simon removed his purse and tipped a handful of golden guineas into the man's hand. 'Then this is some recompense for the work you've been doing. I'm opening the house for the Season and Lady Emily is to have her come out in May. I'm intending to bring up my staff from Sawsbury but would like you and your wife and family to continue working here.'

The man was staring in bewilderment at the coins. 'I've not seen so much in one place in my entire life, my lord.'

Simon became aware they were being watched from the shadows at the far side of the entrance hall. 'Come forward, I wish to make your acquaintance.' He should have known the name of the caretakers and felt ashamed that he didn't.

The woman who came forward smiled shyly and curtsied. Standing behind her were their children who appeared to range from nine or ten up to fifteen or sixteen.

'This is my wife, Maisie Smith, my lord.' Smith said proudly. Then in turn he introduced his family. They were all clean and tidily dressed and he was impressed by their appearance and demeanour.

'Your oldest boy can be a senior footman, the youngest two can work in the kitchen and your girls will make excellent maids. Mrs Smith, are you prepared to stand as housekeeper for the Season and Smith, will you be butler?'

If he had suggested they grew wings

and flew across the hall they could not have looked more astonished.

'My lord, my wife and I are honoured to be offered these positions but . . . '

'If you have kept this house in good heart for years then not only am I grateful, I am also impressed with your diligence and ingenuity. I'll not brook a refusal. I have a cook and four experienced servants coming from Sawsbury and you can learn everything you need to know from them before the house is opened in four weeks or so.'

Smith bowed and his wife curtsied; their progeny followed suit. The new housekeeper stepped forward looking more confident than her husband by her elevation. 'My lord, the master suite is always kept in readiness. Fresh linen was placed on the bed yesterday and the fire has been burning since this morning. Hot water will be brought up to you immediately.'

He nodded his thanks and left them to sort themselves out. The last time the house had been opened there had been a dozen footmen, at least the same number of maids, plus those that worked in the kitchens and stables. No doubt there would be uniforms and suitable gowns for the family somewhere on the premises.

It occurred to him as he entered his apartment that there was unlikely to be anything in the house to feed him. When Mason arrived from his duties in the stables he would send him to speak to the housekeeper. He would have some time to wait as his man knew better than to appear smelling of the stable.

Both the sitting room and bedchamber were warm enough for him — he disliked overheated rooms. This was the first time he had used these chambers and was examining the furniture when he heard the sound of movement in the dressing room. He continued his exploration for a further quarter of an hour, allowing whoever it was to depart without being obliged to bow and scrape to him.

Expecting to find only his hot water,

he was astonished to see that the empty shelves of the large closet now contained not only shirts, but crisply starched neckcloths, two pairs of breeches, two waistcoats and a topcoat that had definitely come from Weston's.

Intrigued, he went to examine them more closely. Of course! These were his own garments that had been abandoned here several years ago. If anything, he was leaner than he had been then and certainly no taller, so they should be a reasonable fit.

He stripped and was in the middle of his ablutions when to his surprise his valet appeared.

'One of the lads prefers to be outside, my lord, so he's acting as groom.'

'Where are you positioned?'

'I've a room downstairs, sir, and I share a parlour with Mr and Mrs Smith.'

'Excellent; this means I'll be able to contact you easily. No doubt they told you of their new positions in the household.'

'They did, my lord, and I'm certain you made the right choice. In the time it took me to wash up . . . ' He stopped as he saw the fresh garments.

'They were mine from some years ago but none the worse for that.'

Mason carefully put out the shaving items and other toiletries, but the saddlebags appeared empty of anything else.

'Mrs Smith has set one of the girls to pressing your clean shirt and stock.'

'I can dress myself; I need you to take a message to Smith. I'll dine at my club tonight. I don't expect them to provide me with dinner at such short notice.'

'I doubt that your evening clothes will have arrived in time for you to change, my lord.'

'Then I'll be obliged to remain in this evening, but ensure they know I need nothing elaborate to eat.'

Freshly garbed and well-satisfied with his restored appearance, Simon headed for the study as there were one or two letters he needed to write and have delivered before the day was out. Being seen at White's in St James's Street this afternoon would give him the opportunity to let the *ton* know he intended to be in Town for the Season. He would mention he was bringing out his sister and that there would be a ball in the first week of May. This should bring forth a plethora of invitations to the most prestigious events.

He might be impoverished but from outward appearances one would not suspect how dire his circumstances were. The house in Grosvenor Square was in good repair — no doubt his father would have sold it if it was not entailed to the estate. There were no outstanding debts to anyone but the bank and it was in their interest to remain silent about these.

It was not far from his house to his club and he would enjoy the walk. The city did not smell so unpleasant in the winter months although the air was always redolent of soot and smoke. He much preferred the country and he

sincerely hoped he would find himself a
bride who didn't wish to spend every
Season in London.

★　★　★

Bella took an instant dislike to Lady
Jones. From the top of her elegantly-
coiffed, pale gold hair to the tip of her
immaculately-shod feet she exuded the
unpleasant attitudes associated with
those of her class. She was arrogant,
patronising and treated the servants as
if they were lesser mortals. The wretched
woman was charm itself when her parents were there, however, when they
were alone her attitude and demeanour
changed.

Two days after this awful person's
arrival, matters came to a dramatic
head. Lady Jones had examined her
wardrobe and, having been unable to
find anything to criticise, she turned her
attention to Bella's appearance and behaviour. The more she spoke, the more
incensed she became.

'I cannot imagine why you think yourself a suitable bride for any member of the aristocracy, Miss Burgoyne. You might be well-educated, your manners are pretty enough, but you have far too much to say for yourself and your complexion is that of a servant.'

'And you, ma'am, are the most unpleasant person I've ever encountered. You are dismissed from my employment. You will leave this house immediately.'

Instead of being confounded by this dismissal, the woman smiled in a supercilious fashion. 'I am your companion, your mentor and cannot be dismissed by you. You will apologise immediately for your appalling impertinence or I shall be speaking to your father.'

This was the outside of enough. 'I think you have misunderstood the situation, ma'am. You are here at my convenience, not yours. I suggest you set your maid to pack your trunks.'

Bella stalked out, then picked up her skirts and ran pell-mell through the house to skid to a halt in the study, where her parents were happily conversing on their forthcoming move to London.

'I have terminated that woman's employment. I will not have her anywhere near me. She is under the erroneous belief that whatever I say you will retain her services.'

Her papa was on his feet at once. 'My dear girl, what has she done to upset you?'

When she explained, his expression changed from benevolent to hard. 'Remain here, my love, I shall see her gone. She came highly recommended, but we should have allowed you to meet her first before offering her employment.'

Bella collapsed on the nearest chair and blinked away unwanted tears. 'Mama, if she is so well connected then she could ruin my chances of finding a husband. I wish I'd held my tongue . . . '

'No, my love, do not blame yourself. Your papa will smooth things over and then we must set about finding another sponsor for you.'

'I don't require one, just a chaperone.

We must depart for London immediately. I'm sure we'll find someone once we're there. I believe there are agencies who deal with this sort of thing. There must be dozens of genteel ladies who would be eager to introduce me into Society.'

Her father returned and smiled encouragingly. 'That woman showed her true colours to me. I cannot believe I was so hoodwinked by her. She is being transported to the nearest inn and from there will travel post-chaise. I was tempted to put her on the common stage but thought that might be taking matters too far.'

She was relieved he hadn't made the horrible woman go on the stage coach — her ladyship was already a formidable enemy and insulting her like that would have made matters so much worse. When he heard Bella's suggestion that they leave as soon as could be arranged, he agreed. He sent a letter by express to warn the staff he had employed for the Season to have the rented house ready for their arrival the following day.

It was no more than three hours to Grosvenor Square and the journey could be accomplished in the morning without the necessity of stopping to rest the horses or take refreshments. The trunks, their personal servants and other necessities left at dawn the following day. She and her parents set off mid-morning in the luxurious carriage Papa had recently acquired, which was drawn by four matching greys.

As she watched the countryside roll by, she wondered if the next time she saw her home she would be betrothed to someone. Would whoever it was want a short engagement?

'Papa, what if the aristocrat who offers for me wishes to be married at once because their finances are in desperate need of your money?'

'Do not fret, my dear girl; things can be arranged to accommodate whatever suits you best. If you require a few months to get to know your future husband before you tie the knot, then so be it. I'm certain that no gentleman would refuse as long as his debts were paid and his coffers filled immediately.'

'That's all very well, but what if I later decide that we don't suit? How will you recover your money?'

'Do you think me a nincompoop, daughter? You can be very sure no money will change hands unless I'm absolutely certain the wedding will go ahead.'

There was little point in pursuing this line of conversation. The onus was on her to make the right choice in the first place. She refused to contemplate the notion that it was the gentleman in question who would do the choosing and not herself.

On the previous occasions that she had visited the metropolis, they had stayed at Grillon's Hotel and not bothered to take a house. Therefore, she was familiar with London and had visited all the sights, ridden in Rotten Row, visited the museums and the opera. She grimaced when she recalled that evening; listening to the singers screeching and yowling reminded her of the farmyard cats when they were fighting.

She was all eagerness to see their new abode when the carriage turned into Grosvenor Square. 'Good heavens, Fredrick, I had no idea all the residences would be of such modern construction. How splendid they are and how large is the square itself! I'm sure we shall be very happy here.'

The carriage rolled to a standstill outside a large, four-storey edifice and immediately a pair of footmen in bright blue livery and gold frogging dashed from the front door to let down the steps and hand them out.

'Look, Mama, there's a small park in which we can take a constitutional each morning in the centre of the square. However, the houses are joined together and I'm not sure that I approve of that.'

Her father chuckled. 'I can assure you this house is palatial inside and has an excellent trio of reception rooms as well as a ballroom. No doubt you're wondering where our carriage and horses are to go.'

They were now standing in front of the smart black railings which enclosed a small area of frontage. He gestured to the end of the row and, by stepping into the road, she saw that there was an archway.

'I can see the entrance to the stables is further along. Mama, we must remember to allow extra time for the horses to be put to. Will there be a mount for me to ride?'

'I thought you might like me to attend Tattersalls and choose for you, my love.'

'I should like that above anything, Papa. Am I permitted to walk in the park without a maid in attendance?'

'I see no reason why not; there are several young ladies doing so, as well as nursemaids with their young charges. The weather is surprisingly clement for the time of year so you'll come to no harm for an hour.'

Her parents vanished into the house and the door closed behind them and the footmen. It would seem she would have to knock on the door when she was ready to enter. After spending a pleasant time stretching her legs and admiring the scenery, she decided to venture further afield and look at some of the grander houses on the other side of the square.

Her view was obscured by high hedges but she discovered there was a gate that led from the central garden onto the road that ran around the square. So engrossed was she in her study of the building that she neglected to look in either direction to see if there was a vehicle or horseman approaching.

# 3

Simon emerged from his front door and strode down the path. As he was exiting, a pigeon flapped noisily above him and he instinctively looked up. He stepped into the road with his eyes on the roof, colliding with a young lady who was staring at the gargoyles that adorned the gutter on his house.

He grabbed her arms and for a few seconds they rocked back and forth in danger of ending on their backsides. Her bonnet was now over one eye and his beaver was the other side of the road.

'What the devil do you think you were doing? You could have caused us both serious damage.' As he was admonishing the girl, without conscious thought, he reached out and straightened her hat. She raised her head and he was looking into the most beautiful pair of emerald-green eyes he had ever seen.

'Kindly release me at once, sir. I do not take kindly to being manhandled. If you had not been gawping in the wrong direction, this accident would not have taken place.'

He dropped his hands and couldn't prevent his smile. 'Touché, ma'am; I think we're both culpable. Forgive me, I must recover my hat.'

He turned, and at that precise moment a carriage bowled past, crushing his headgear beneath its wheels. He would not have been so cross if she had not laughed.

'I think your hat is done for, sir. Perhaps that will make you more observant when you exit your house next time.'

Before he could think of a pithy response, she dipped in a curtsy and ran lightly across the road and back through the gate. As the hedges were high along this side of the garden, he had no idea in which direction she went once she was out of sight.

He hurried across, picked up his ruined beaver and stepped into the park. There was no sign of her and he cursed under his breath. She must be resident here: she was dressed fashionably, spoke as one would expect and he was determined to discover her identity and further his acquaintance.

Without the required headgear, he could not continue his walk; he must return home and find a replacement. With luck, Smith or his wife would know who the young lady was. He paused as he reached the magnificent frontage. His town house was one of the largest in the square and had been built by his grandfather on his return from India. It was more than three times the size of those terraced residences on the other side of the gardens — but all in Grosvenor Square were prestigious homes and only the wealthiest could afford to either rent or own one.

Mason shook his head sadly when he was handed the hat. 'I fear this is beyond redemption, my lord, and your other one is somewhat moth-eaten.'

'I've no choice; if I'm to go out to my club as planned, I'll have to wear it. Explaining to my acquaintances the reason for my appearing with such a disgraceful object should cause much merriment.'

Simon trusted his valet's total discretion and therefore explained his desire to know the identity of the girl who had caused the demise of his headgear.

'I hope to have the information you require on your return, my lord.'

Smith was waiting to speak to him on his descent. The change in his appearance was remarkable — he was now dressed from head to toe in regulation black and looked every inch a butler. 'My lord, I have reopened the accounts at the establishments that were used in the past. I hope this meets with your approval.'

'I'm surprised you knew which ones they were, but I trust you to manage these matters for me. Another thing: I have sent word to Lady Emily asking her to come at once. I don't intend to return to Sawsbury. The house is fit to live in without the necessity of extensive refurbishment so I can see no reason to delay the transfer of our household.'

'Yes, my lord. Might I be permitted to enquire if you will be requiring guest rooms and other chambers to be prepared as well?'

For a moment Simon was mystified by this question and then he understood the significance of the remark. Smith would be expecting that there would be a respectable matron as part of the party. As yet he had not appointed a suitable chaperone and companion for his sister. He could not be expected to dance attendance on her everywhere she wished to go and she could hardly gallivant about the place with only a maid and footman to attend her.

'Prepare both family apartments.' Another urgent reason for visiting White's was now to get a recommendation for a suitable chaperone for Emily.

Smith bowed and stepped aside. His oldest son, now appropriately dressed in green livery, was there to open the door for Simon. He turned and called to the butler.

'I'm happy for your younger son to work in the stables if that's what he prefers to do.'

'Thank you, my lord.'

The brisk walk helped him to clear his head. His hat was under his arm; its dilapidated state was less evident there. He signed in on his arrival at White's as this gave him the opportunity to scan the other names and see if there was anyone here that he knew.

Afternoons were usually quiet: the club became busier at night. He noted one friend was here and went in search of him. He had handed in his hat, gloves and cane and was still smiling at the look of horror on the doorman's face when he strolled into the room that faced St James's Street. The person he sought was sitting in the bay window, watching the pedestrians walk past in the hope of seeing an attractive young lady he could ogle.

'Featherstone, I might have guessed I'd find you sitting here.'

The young man turned, and seeing who it was leapt to his feet with a genuine smile of welcome. 'Tarnation take it! I'd no idea you were up in Town. Well met, Sawsbury. Are you out of mourning now?'

They shook hands and then took seats away from the window where they could converse privately. 'The year was up in January. My sister is to have her debut — she missed out last year because of our father's unexpected demise. I'd be grateful if you would spread the word that we're here as I want her to attend as many functions as possible.'

'Happy to, old fellow. I'm obliged to become leg-shackled this year. The pater is threatening to cut off my allowance if I don't find myself a bride.' He beckoned over a hovering footman and ordered coffee. 'I expect you're on the lookout too.'

'You know my views on matrimony, my friend, but I am, like you, five and twenty and should not leave it much longer to start filling my nursery.'

They chatted companionably about the end of the war and the incarceration of Bonaparte, the high price of corn and the problems facing those without regular employment in the countryside. Then, coffee finished, he remembered he also wanted a recommendation for a chaperone for his sister.

Featherstone banged the table, making the cups jump and two elderly gentlemen glare at them. 'What a stroke of luck for both of us. My Aunt Jemima returned from her travels and asked me that very thing this morning.'

'I assume that you mean she's looking for a temporary position of the kind that I just spoke of?'

'Didn't I just say so? Aunt Jemima was married to my uncle; you will recall that he was a Colonel in the Light Brigade. Well, he died at Salamanca or some such place and now she's eager to find something to do.'

Simon had been at Oxford with Featherstone and was quite fond of him. He was a genial fellow, but not famous for his intelligence. 'Is this determination to find employment because she has been left without funds?'

His friend looked bemused at the question. 'Devil take it, Sawsbury, I thought you were a clever fellow. I just told you: she's bored with civilian life, and she remained with his regiment until the war was over. She only returned a few weeks ago and finds life exceedingly dull after all the excitement.'

There was little point in saying that he'd said nothing of the kind. 'I see. If she spent the last few years following the drum I can't see that she'll have the right credentials and be able to obtain invitations and vouchers for my sister.'

'She's Lady Jemima Featherstone, the daughter of some earl or other, as well as the widow of my uncle who was a Colonel, Lord Edward Featherstone. She knows everyone who matters.' He surged to his feet and grabbed Simon by the shoulder. 'Come with me now and meet her.'

* * *

Bella guessed the very large, extremely attractive gentleman would come in search of her, so dashed though the nearest gate on the other side of the gardens and pressed herself up against the railing. She heard him on the other side, but he didn't look over the hedge, and a few moments later he departed.

She ran back to her own house and was delighted, but surprised, when the door opened as she arrived. She smiled her thanks and stepped inside what was to be her home for the next few months. Papa was right to say the house was far more palatial than was apparent from the front.

The entrance hall was the full width of the building and the length was double that. The smart black and white marble tiles set off the grand staircase admirably. She walked into the drawing room and again was impressed by not only the size, but the excellent furniture and decorations.

She would leave further exploration of the ground floor until after she had refreshed herself from the journey. She asked to be directed to her own apartment and the footman took her up himself.

'These are your chambers, Miss Burgoyne. The door opposite leads to Mrs Burgoyne's sitting room. Is there anything else you require?'

She shook her head and stepped into her new abode. Her own sitting room had everything she wanted and more. There was a small desk fully equipped with ink, paper and quills. The bookshelf was overflowing but on examination she found none of the volumes to her liking. The sermons, travel guides and books on flora and fauna would remain unread.

It hardly seemed worth the effort to change her gown when she had only been wearing it for a few hours, but it was a travelling ensemble and if she was to conform with what was expected, she must now put on a morning gown.

Her maid had put out another new dress, this one mint green with darker green embroidery and sash; there was also a spencer and reticule made from the same material and decorated in the same way. The slippers were dyed to match.

She completed her ablutions quickly, stepped into the necessary underpinnings and then barely restrained her impatience whilst her hair was tidied.

'Do you require anything else, Miss Burgoyne?'

'No, I'll not need you until I'm obliged to change for dinner later.'

She picked up her skirt and rushed through the house and went in search of her parents who had established themselves in a smaller reception room that overlooked the little garden at the back.

'There you are, my love. Did you enjoy your promenade?'

She told them what had transpired and they laughed. 'I have a list of the names of those who own houses on that side of the square in my study. Would you like me to find it so you know the name of this gentleman?'

'No thank you, Papa. He was an irascible gentleman, although I'm forced to admit he was a prodigiously handsome one too.'

Her father chuckled and went in search of his list. He guessed her protestations were false. 'Mama, what are we to do about my lack of a sponsor?'

'We have been discussing exactly that and have concluded that we shall manage very well without one. There's no urgency in our search for a suitable husband for you. Lord Danbury is calling here later today and I'm sure that Lady Danbury will be happy to escort you anywhere her two girls are going.'

'Then why did Papa think it necessary to appoint that obnoxious woman?'

'You know your father, my love; he wants only the best for you and believed such a person would benefit your introduction to the *ton*. I just hope that woman does not ruin your chances of being accepted by spreading malicious and untrue rumours about us.'

'There's nothing we can do about it, Mama, so we must put it from our minds and concentrate on what we can do. Have your cards been sent out to all the houses in the square?'

'Oh no, that would be presumptuous of me . . . '

'It would be nothing of the kind. How will anyone know we're here if you don't inform them? What's the worst that could happen?' This was a rhetorical question and she continued without waiting for an answer. 'If you receive morning calls tomorrow afternoon and cards from them then you will know you have been accepted.'

Her father strolled in and heard her last remark. 'And what do we do, Bella, if your mama's cards are ignored?'

'There's nothing we can do but hope Lady Danbury's approval will rectify matters. I suppose we could always put an advert in The Times — ask any impoverished aristocrat to apply directly for my hand and thus cut out the nonsense of attending Almack's and numerous events in order to get noticed.'

Her father knew at once she was jesting but her mother thought for a second this suggestion was genuine and went quite pale. They were still laughing together when Lord and Lady Danbury were announced.

A tall, spare gentleman of middle years and florid complexion walked in, closely followed by his wife. Lady Danbury was small, rounded and was smiling and looking around with interest.

'Good afternoon, my lady, my lord. Thank you for coming. Allow me to present my wife and my daughter, Annabel.'

Bella curtsied, as did her mother, and Lady Danbury immediately rushed forward shaking her head. 'No, no, I will not stand on ceremony with you. You must not curtsy to me; my parents were in trade as you are and I know exactly how you must feel.'

Papa led his lordship away, no doubt to discuss business, and left them to talk amongst themselves. 'Bella, will you ring for refreshments?'

She did so and then sat beside her mother, eager to hear more from this charming and unpretentious lady.

'I did not bring my girls today, but you will meet them when you come to supper tomorrow. We are in Hanover Square, no more than five minutes from here. My daughters, Sarah and Elizabeth, are twins, have just reached their eighteenth anniversary, and if my husband had his way they would be made to wait another year for their come out. He has no wish for them to marry and leave us.'

'My lady, I cannot wait to meet them. Do they ride?'

'No, they dislike anything energetic apart from dancing. However, they will be happy to accompany you to Hatchards bookshop or to Gunter's for an ice.'

Bella noticed that Papa had left the list he'd gone to fetch on a side table. She politely excused herself and took it to the window to read, leaving the two matrons to a comfortable coze. Small wonder Lord Danbury had become a close friend of Papa's; he had happily married out of his class as she hoped to do.

As she walked to the window she glanced over her shoulder. From the lively conversation taking place between her mother and her new friend, she was certain that before Lady Danbury departed Mama would be fully cognizant of the circumstances that saw Lord Danbury marry to his disadvantage.

She ran her eye down the list until she came to the grand houses that stood alone. The one from which the unknown gentleman had emerged was Sawsbury House and presumably he was Lord Sawsbury. From the appearance of the house, and his lordship, he wouldn't be looking for an heiress — for all she knew he was already married.

'My lady,' she called, interrupting the conversation before she realised how impolite this was. 'Can you tell me anything about the occupants of Sawsbury House?'

'Come and join us and I will tell you everything I know. His papa, the previous Lord Sawsbury, was killed in a shooting accident just over a year ago. Lady Emily, the new lord's sister, might well have her come out this year.'

'Then I'll hope to make her acquaintance in due course. Mama, did you regale her ladyship with our unfortunate encounter with Lady Jones?'

'I have yet to do so. Listen, I can hear the tea tray coming — can I leave you to deal with that, my dear?'

Lady Danbury and her husband stayed for more than an hour and everyone was well-satisfied with the encounter. Bella was eagerly anticipating meeting Elizabeth and Sarah the following morning when they were to walk together along Bond Street.

When she was about to climb into bed, she heard the sound of raised voices coming from the other side of

the square. Her bedchamber overlooked the communal gardens; sound
travels wonderfully well at night.

She moved swiftly to the window,
making sure she could not be seen, and
listened to the altercation.

# 4

Simon appointed Featherstone's aunt without hesitation. There was no need to consult his sister as he was certain she would approve. Having achieved both his aims, one to appoint a suitable chaperone and the other to be seen about Town, he was happy to acquiesce to his friend's cajoling that they go to watch a curricle race in which several young bucks were taking part. This was to be run in Green Park, no distance from Grosvenor Square, which would mean he could return home easily enough when the race was done.

'It will be capital fun, Sawsbury, and then you can invite the participants to your house for a few drinks to celebrate.'

'I'll do no such thing, I only arrived today and my staff are not ready for such an invasion. I'm sure we can find somewhere else. If we cut down Queen's

Walk we'll be in Piccadilly and can go to Pulteney's Hotel in Bolton Street.'

'Excellent notion, old fellow. They won't give a fig for us not being changed for the evening.'

On the way there, it occurred to Simon that half a dozen curricles would not be welcome in that part of town. 'I assume that the drivers of these vehicles will have grooms to take their curricles home?'

'No idea. But knowing them, they'll expect to bring them to the hotel.'

They arrived at Green Park to find a small crowd of eager spectators waiting to see the race. Wagers were being made on the outcome for extraordinary amounts of money, but gambling was not something he approved of after the way it had destroyed his father and his family's finances.

The crowd of young gentlemen became rowdier as they drank constantly from their hip flasks. Featherstone had wandered off to talk to one of the racers, which gave him the opportunity to drift away unnoticed. These young men were of the same generation as he, but he was no longer comfortable as part of this crowd. No doubt they too would be bowed down with responsibilities in the next few years so he didn't begrudge them their harmless enjoyment.

He heard the cheers as the race began and prayed that no one would come to grief. He strolled back to his dwelling and this time decided to enter through the stables, as the archway that led behind the house was closer than going to the front door.

His horses were comfortable, the carriage already pristine, and he went inside satisfied with the day. Smith met him as he emerged into the hall.

'Good evening, my lord, I thought you might like to dine in the rose room this evening.'

'I'd be quite happy with a tray in the library, Smith, there's no need to go to any fuss.'

'Your cook arrived, along with your luggage and other staff, and she has already prepared an excellent repast for you.'

'In which case, I'll be down shortly to eat.'

The meal was excellent and he drank rather too much claret with it. Mason had not discovered the identity of the young lady but was certain that she lived opposite, in a house that was rented for the Season.

He settled in front of the fire in the library, which had always been his favourite room, and made considerable inroads into a decanter of excellent cognac. He was thinking of retiring when there was a racket outside and a hammering on the front door.

Who the hell was this? He decided he should investigate himself, despite the fact that he kept staff to do this for him. His butler was standing in front of the closed door, holding a conversation with those outside.

'Lord Sawsbury has retired. I suggest that you call tomorrow, sirs, and cease disturbing the neighbourhood with your noise.'

'Thank you, Smith, I know who it is. I'll get rid of them myself. Open the door enough for me to slip out and then close it immediately behind me.'

As expected, he found a small crowd of very inebriated gentlemen gathered on his doorstep. They were demanding to be let in to continue the party. They were led by his friend who was the most raucous of them all.

'There you are, about time too. We've been banging on your door this age. You invited us round and now are refusing us entry . . . '

Simon took Featherstone's arm, turned him round briskly, and marched him back into the street. His cronies had no option but to follow. 'You're drunk as a wheelbarrow, my friend, and making a spectacle of yourself. Kindly go home and take your acquaintances with you before you have the whole square out here demanding to know what the commotion is.'

His friend stared at him, his expression confused. Then he beamed. 'Can't we come in for a drink or two before we go?'

'You cannot. You were supposed to be going to Bolton Street; I suggest you go there now and let the residents of Grosvenor Square return to their slumber.'

All might have been well if it hadn't been for one of the party, who became more demanding. 'Featherstone said we were invited here and I ain't going nowhere without a drink.'

'You will leave immediately unless you wish for unpleasant repercussions.' Simon had intended his remark to send them on their way but the gentleman he had spoken to became belligerent.

'I told you, whoever you are, we ain't moving. Lord Sawsbury . . . '

'I am Lord Sawsbury and you will leave this neighbourhood immediately or will regret it in the morning.'

He stepped in fast, using his height and weight to intimidate. It did the reverse and the wretched fellow took a swing at him. Fortunately, the man was so bosky his aim was bad, but this was the signal for the rest to join in.

The unwanted visitors began fighting each other. There was little he could do about it, as he had no intention of becoming involved. He stepped back into his own domain and firmly closed the gates.

The blows rarely landed and he was sure the fisticuffs would stop of their own accord. Then lights began to come on, front doors opened and suddenly the square was full of footmen sent out to remove the noisy, drunken rabble.

The identities of those involved would be noted — servants knew everyone — and they would be *persona non grata* in many drawing rooms once word had spread about their appalling behaviour. He grabbed Featherstone's arm and bundled him back up the steps. Smith had the door open in a flash.

'Leave him to me, my lord, I'll get him settled in a guest room where he can sleep it off.'

Bella became so engrossed in the fracas that was growing in volume outside Lord Sawsbury's house that she stretched out and carefully pushed up the window so she could both see and hear more of what was going on.

In the flickering light of the flambeaux that burnt outside the house she could clearly see a group of drunken young men staggering about, whilst one of them hammered on his door and demanded to be let in. She watched with interest as the gentleman in question came out and moved the group from his premises into the road.

When the fisticuffs started, she could hardly contain her amusement as the fighters swung and missed on most occasions. Then lights came on in several of the houses and a positive army of footmen, most of them correctly dressed, rushed out and bundled the young men from the square.

His    lordship    had    very    sensibly

retreated, taking one of the participants with him. Presumably this was a friend of his who he didn't wish to be associated with the inevitable disgrace that would follow this debacle.

Where these young men had come from and why they were so inebriated she had no idea — but she was determined to find out on the morrow. She tumbled into bed and did not wake until she was roused by her maid with her morning chocolate and sweet rolls.

It was but a short walk along Brook Street to Hanover Square where she and her mama were to meet up with Lady Danbury and her daughters before continuing into Bond Street. This road was the grand mart for fashionable items of dress and was the resort of ladies of the *ton*.

They were seen as they approached and the three ladies came out of their house to greet them. 'My dear Mrs Burgoyne, Miss Burgoyne, we shall not dally here but go at once to New Bond Street. This is my Sarah and this Elizabeth.'

Lady Danbury waved vaguely at the two girls who were only distinguishable because one was wearing a blue ribbon on her bonnet and the other a green.

The matrons bustled on ahead, leaving Bella to make friends as best she could with these two fashionable young ladies. 'Please, which of you is wearing green and which blue?'

The young lady with the blue ribbon smiled. 'I'm Sarah. I always wear blue and Beth always wears green.' She smiled mischievously. 'Although, it has been known for us to confuse our dearest parents by reversing this.'

'It must be such fun being a twin. I have no other siblings — indeed, I had no friends of my own age at all until now.'

Beth linked arms with her and shook her head at this depressing news. 'Why is that? Surely there are families in the neighbourhood you could mix with?'

Before Bella could answer, Sarah, who was now holding her other arm, did so for her. 'You know how it is, sister: the aristocracy have no time for anyone but their own class. I expect your nearest neighbours think themselves too grand for you.'

'Exactly so. I wish my parents hadn't decided to buy such a vast estate; things would have been quite different. Gentlefolk are not so fussy about such things.'

'Mama insists that you come back for luncheon and she can give you a dozen or more invitation cards she has obtained from friends. I don't suppose you have vouchers for Almack's?'

'I don't, but that place is only for young ladies with impeccable pedigrees. It sounds an insipid sort of event, and not somewhere I wish to go.'

Sarah giggled. 'The refreshments are indifferent, there's no alcohol served and gentlemen are not admitted unless wearing knee breeches and stockings. I much prefer to see a gentleman in trousers and evening slippers, don't you?'

'My experience of such things is very limited — I hope you will still wish to be my friend when I tell you I've only attended one assembly in my entire life.'

'How sad! I can assure you that our mama intends to change all that. You are so beautiful, your hair is the colour of autumn leaves and your eyes sparkle like emeralds. Your ensemble is the height of fashion and suits you to perfection.' Beth patted her hand. 'The fact that you are a substantial heiress as well will more than make up for your family.'

'How true, sister. Being beautiful and rich will make you popular with those not bothered by your birth.'

Bella snatched her arms away, stopped where she was and looked at both girls with disfavour. 'I find I have the head-ache. Please tell my mother I've returned home.' She turned and dashed off before they could protest.

\* \* \*

Simon discovered a very repentant Featherstone waiting for him when he descended the following morning.

71

'I apologise most humbly for bringing that rabble to your door last night, Sawsbury. The pater would not have been impressed if I'd been found amongst them. So, I must also thank you for your timely intervention.'

'Think nothing of it, my friend. It will not go so well for you or your cronies if it occurs a second time. Do I make myself clear?'

'Perfectly. Forgive me if I don't join you to break my fast. I must return home and get out of my dirt. I can assure you that I'll not forget your help.'

His friend sloped off through the stables and thence down the tradesmen's passages so he would not be seen exiting the house where the disturbance had taken place the previous night. Emily should be arriving today, or tomorrow morning at the latest. Featherstone's Aunt Jemima would also be here later, so if he intended to take a constitutional, he had better do it now. His riding horse had yet to arrive.

He had not got to bed until the small

hours and this morning had risen later than his usual seven o'clock. By the time he'd breakfasted it was mid-morning. Mason handed him his dilapidated hat.

'No, I refuse to wear that or even to carry it under my arm. I'll not take my gloves or cane either.'

The weather was clement for the beginning of spring and in his own gardens at the rear of the building there were daffodils and other blooms, blue ones that he did not know the name of, giving a welcome patch of colour in the empty beds.

The problem with not wearing a hat was that he couldn't tip it to acknowledge a greeting; instead, he was constantly nodding and smiling at those that thought they might know him. He was surprised how busy the thoroughfares were with pedestrians eager to visit the splendid emporiums that lined New Bond Street.

His walk was uneventful until he saw a group of young men emerge from

Gentleman John Jackson's Gymnasium and accost a young lady who was, inexplicably, unaccompanied by either maid or footman.

He increased his pace and arrived at her side before anything untoward could take place. He recognised her immediately as the young lady he'd collided with yesterday. 'My dear, forgive me for dawdling; I should have remained at your side.' He smiled at her and she immediately played along.

'My dear Lord Sawsbury, no apologies are necessary. I should have realised I had walked on alone.'

Simon fixed the three dandies with an arctic stare. He had no need to do more as the mention of his name as much as his formidable size caused them to back away, apologising profusely as they did so for behaving so rudely.

Once they were alone, he put his other hand over hers, thus preventing her from escaping. 'You have the advantage of me.'

'I am Miss Annabel Burgoyne and I

thank you for your timely intervention, my lord. I was so angered by something my companions said that I dashed off, but I now discover it was in entirely the wrong direction.'

'Allow me to escort you home, Miss Burgoyne.' He looked around in an ostentatious fashion. 'Your servants? Are they hiding somewhere I cannot see them?'

She laughed and did not take offence. 'As you very well know, my lord, I'm unaccompanied. I was walking with Lady Danbury and her daughters, as well as my own mama, in New Bond Street, so there was no necessity to bring my maid with me.'

'I suppose I should not be surprised that you have a quick temper — russet hair and green eyes, I believe, are the usual indication.'

'So I'm told, sir, but I can assure you I'm usually the most amiable of creatures. I rarely raise my voice and am famous for my patience under all circumstances.'

'And I don't believe a word of it. Tell

me, what so incensed you that you forgot not only your sense of direction but also your sense of propriety?'

'I'm not sure that this is any of your concern, my lord. I should like to know, however, why those noisy gentlemen were hammering on your door last night.'

When he explained to her the circumstances, she told him she was impressed that he had had the forethought to remove his friend before the neighbours sent their servants out.

'If I had known there was a curricle race I might well have joined you to watch.'

'You would have done no such thing, Miss Burgoyne. You obviously have no notion of what is acceptable behaviour for a young lady. I must suppose that's because this is your first visit to Town.'

He'd seen several heads turning as they strolled past arm in arm, without a chaperone in sight. By rescuing her, he might well have caused further damage to her precarious reputation.

'Miss Burgoyne, you're unfamiliar with London society. For an unmarried young lady to be seen unaccompanied in Bond Street could give rise to unpleasant speculation. However, being seen walking with me might well be even more damaging.'

'I don't give a fig for my reputation. I think the rules that govern your so-called society are both restrictive and unkind. I'll tell you why I was angry: Lady Danbury's daughters told me that my looks and wealth might almost compensate for my lack of breeding.'

His pulse quickened. Could it be that by some strange quirk of fate he had met exactly the young lady he'd come up to Town to discover?

'Forgive me for asking such a personal question, but are you here to find yourself a husband?'

She detected something in his query and looked up at him, her eyes wide. Was she thinking the same thing as him?

'Then I shall ask you something impertinent in my turn, my lord. Are you an impecunious aristocrat in search of an heiress?'

He drew her into the privacy of an archway before answering. 'I am indeed. Do you think you might be the bride I seek?'

Her cheeks coloured and she trembled. 'I think it's entirely possible, my lord, that our fortuitous meetings might have saved us both a deal of unnecessary parading in overheated ballrooms with unwashed and over-perfumed guests.'

'We've yet to be formally introduced so I can hardly speak to your father until we have.'

'We cannot linger here, my lord; we're drawing unwanted attention to ourselves.'

'As I'm hoping that we can announce our betrothal by the end of the day, I hardly think it matters.'

Her laugh was delightful but turned several heads in their direction. Young ladies of decorum didn't laugh out loud in public.

'My lord, I think you're ahead of

yourself on this matter. Admittedly you're exactly what I had in mind for myself, but I think we should get to know each other a little better before we make a lifetime commitment, however convenient it might seem.'

'I am five and twenty, have no vices, and am only in this position because of my father's gambling. I have a sister, Emily, who is nineteen years old and as far as the *ton* is concerned I'm here to find her a husband. She is to have her debut ball in May.'

'I am the same age as Lady Emily, my parents have always wished me to marry well, but the decision as to who I choose will be left to me.'

'She will be here later today or first thing tomorrow. If your mama leaves her card then we can call tomorrow afternoon without raising eyebrows. On reflection, I think it might be better if we keep our plans to ourselves for the moment.'

Her gurgle of laughter made him smile in return. 'I wasn't aware, sir, that we had any plans. All that has transpired as far as I'm concerned is that we've both admitted we're looking for a partner and that it's possible we might suit.'

'I hesitate to disagree with you so early in our acquaintance, Miss Burgoyne, but I believe it was you who said our meeting had saved us both the bother of attending balls and soirées in order to find a suitable partner.'

'*Touché*, my lord. I did indeed say exactly that. You had startled me by your remarks so I spoke without thought. Am I now allowed to retract that statement without causing offence?'

'I'm not so easily dissuaded. The fact that you discovered my name means you were also interested. I made similar enquiries but was not successful. Why should we fight fate? We were literally thrown together yesterday and again today — as far as I'm concerned, my search is over. I shall marry you whether you want me to or not.' His words had tumbled forth of their own volition but he did not regret them. 'In fact, I'm quite prepared to go down on one knee right here in New Bond Street and make you an offer.'

'You'll do no such thing. Anyway, I can see my mama waving to me from across the street so I shall thank you for your assistance and make my farewells.'

# 5

Bella attempted to extricate her arm from his but he was having none of it. She could hardly struggle in so public a place so was obliged to cross the street still attached to him.

'My dear girl, where have you been? Lady Danbury and her daughters were most put out by your sudden disappearance and have continued on their shopping expedition in high dudgeon.' Her mother stared pointedly at her companion.

'Mama, allow me to present to you Lord Sawsbury. You will recall that I met him yesterday outside his house. Today he came to my rescue when I was in a difficult situation.'

Her parent curtsied and smiled politely but did not seem at all overawed by meeting someone so toplofty. 'Thank you, my lord, for bringing my daughter back to me. I am most grateful for your intervention.'

Finally, he allowed her to remove her hand. He nodded politely. 'I'm delighted to meet you, Mrs Burgoyne. As we are almost neighbours I'm certain we shall see more of each other in future.'

He nodded again and then strolled off. The fact that he winked at her before he departed made her heart skip a beat. He really was an attractive gentleman and ticked all the items on her list. Why was she not in high alt at having found exactly the husband she was hoping for?

'Annabel, what were you thinking? If his lordship had not been there to rescue you I shudder to think what could have happened.'

'I apologise, Mama. It was both rude and stupid of me to rush off like that un-escorted. Those silly girls deeply offended me by their thoughtless comments — if you expect me to be bosom bows with them you are going to be disappointed.'

'It would have made your time in London easier, made people more ready to accept you . . . '

'That's exactly why I got so cross. You and Papa are as good as anyone with blue blood and I'll not have anyone imply differently. Papa is where he is today because of his own hard work, he wasn't handed everything on a silver platter like those you wish me to mix with.' As she finished the sentence she understood why she had not been thrilled that Sawsbury wanted to marry her.

'I'm sorry, Mama, but I am no longer sure that I can marry an aristocrat after all, however much you both wish me to. Lord Sawsbury is determined to make me an offer and I should have been pleased because he is everything I thought I wanted in a husband. However . . . '

She was forced to jump aside to avoid being knocked down by a trio of young gentlemen driving curricles with complete disregard to anyone who might be walking in their path. This meant they were obliged to walk single file until they were safely inside their own house.

'Goodness me, Bella, where did all the traffic come from? I thought Grosvenor Square was a select place, yet we were almost killed by those vehicles.'

'I'll explain who they are once we're safely inside. I hope Papa is within as he must be prepared for the arrival of my would-be suitor.'

Once she had handed over her bonnet, pelisse, gloves and reticule to her waiting maid, she went in search of her parents. She hated to disappoint them but they would have to wait for their grandchildren to elevate the family, as she had no intention of doing so.

They listened to her explanation as to why she had changed her mind without comment. It was her father who spoke first.

'I think you're as prejudiced as those you despise. How can you dismiss a person because of their birth without actually talking to them, knowing them? Of course, I agree there are members of the aristocracy I'd not wish to be acquainted with but equally there are members of our class who are equally despicable.'

'My dear, we shall not push you to do something you don't like but why not experience the Season, mingle with the *ton* before you dismiss them all.'

'Mama, I'll do as you ask but I'm certain I wouldn't be happy being the wife of a lord, having nothing better to do than speak to the housekeeper, look at fashion plates and hold supper parties.' No sooner had she spoken than she realised how foolish she was being. The life she described was the one her mother now had and was the kind of life that every young lady aspired to.

'Exactly what do you expect to be doing if you marry someone from the bourgeoisie?'

'It's wealth that makes the difference, not birth — I understand that now. There must be hundreds of genteel young ladies who are impoverished and forced to work for their living and I'm certain they would prefer to be ladies of leisure.'

'Good girl, I see you understand. Why not marry someone with a title if he's a gentleman that you like? Equally, if you find no one you think you will be happy with over these next few weeks then we will widen our search.'

'Thank you for being so understanding, Papa. I think what has caused me to vacillate over this subject is not the thought of marrying out of my class, but marrying without love. I thought I would be content with a business arrangement but now think I will wait until my affections are engaged.'

'In which case, Bella, shall I send this Sawsbury fellow packing when he comes to me?'

'I don't think he will apply to you just yet; he wishes me to meet his sister who is also on the marriage mart this Season. Have your cards been delivered around the square, Mama?'

'A footman is taking them at this very moment. If Lord Sawsbury and his sister come to call this afternoon then I'm sure the others will follow his lead.'

'If you will excuse me, I must write a letter of apology to Lady Danbury. Perhaps the footman can deliver it after he has finished taking the cards.'

It was difficult to compose a letter expressing sentiments she did not feel, but she thought the letter should be enough to smooth things over. Her behaviour had been selfish; her mama had obviously enjoyed the company of Lady Danbury, and Lord Danbury was a personal friend of her father's. She would do nothing further to jeopardise these relationships even if it meant spending more time with Elizabeth and Sarah.

Morning calls, as far as she knew, took place between eleven in the morning and three in the afternoon. It was now a little after midday so it was perfectly possible, but unlikely, that they could receive the first of their visitors at any time.

Bella rarely took an interest in the ensemble she intended to wear. Today was different and she selected a gown of moss-green velvet that had long sleeves and a pretty heart-shaped neckline.

'That looks a picture, miss, it complements your eyes,' her maid said as she shook out the skirt.

'I'll not need to take a wrap which is why I chose it.'

Satisfied she looked her best, she glanced at the overmantel clock. She had taken more than an hour to get ready and this was unheard of. As she hurried towards the stairs she heard voices coming from the drawing room and knew there were already callers. She was tardy and this was not a good first impression to make on her neighbours.

\* \* \*

'Shall we go immediately to visit the Burgoynes, Simon? I've changed my gown, have no wish to eat luncheon and have no need to rest.' Emily moved rapidly towards the front door, leaving Simon no option but to follow.

'I thought tomorrow would be soon enough, I've no wish to appear desperate.'

'That's as may be, but I'm eager to meet this young lady who will shortly become my sister if you have your way.'

He knew when to give in and was certain she would go on her own if he didn't accompany her. 'At least we have received their card. I doubt that anyone else will visit, so we must be as visible as possible as we walk across the square.'

Instead of taking the shortcut through the gardens, they walked around the perimeter; he saw several curtains twitch as they went past. Hopefully, whoever was watching would see them go into the house and be curious enough to follow suit.

Personally, he didn't give a damn that his future wife and her family were cits, but he was determined to make things as easy for her as he could by drawing in the toplofty families who looked down on trade.

'I have their invitation to my come-out ball here and will deliver it myself.'

'Have we had many replies, Emily?'

'A dozen so far and all of them in the affirmative. Don't look back, but three ladies and their daughters are following our lead.'

The door opened as they approached and a smartly dressed footman bowed them in. He then led them across the hall and announced them loudly at the entrance to the drawing room.

To his surprise there were already several visitors. Mrs Burgoyne hurried over to greet him. 'Thank you for coming, my lord, I cannot think why my daughter is so late. I'm certain she will be here shortly. Allow me to introduce you to Lady Danbury and her daughters.'

'First, I'd like you to meet my sister, Lady Emily.'

Introductions over, he wandered off and positioned himself behind a convenient plant. The refreshments being served were better than the usual fare one was offered when making morning calls. There were dainty sandwiches, a selection of small pastries and cakes, as well as both tea and coffee to drink.

He already knew Lady Jamieson and her feckless son — she was obviously on the lookout for an heiress for him. Emily circulated whilst he remained in the shadows where he could watch the door.

A few minutes after his arrival, Annabel came in. He was certain she saw him but instead of greeting him she went immediately to the Danburys. He was pleased that she was obviously smoothing things out after her behaviour this morning.

His sister glided up beside him. 'Come, I wish to be introduced at once.'

He was about to escort her over when his quarry turned and walked towards him. Her smile tilted his world.

'Lord Sawsbury, thank you so much for coming. This must be Lady Emily for there is a strong familial resemblance.' She curtsied, he nodded, but his sister offered both her hands and after a slight hesitation Annabel took them.

'I only arrived a little while ago, Miss

Burgoyne, but could not wait another minute to meet the young lady who has made such an impression on my brother.'

'I'm delighted that you came, my lady . . . '

'No, you must call me Emily and I shall call you Annabel.'

'I would prefer it if you called me Bella; I'm only called by my full name when in disgrace.' Emily delved into her reticule and handed over the invitation.

'Thank you so much for bringing this personally . . . '

Simon's attention was distracted as Lady Jamieson and her son, having stayed the allotted quarter of an hour, were obliged to go without more than a few moments with the young lady they'd come to see. As they departed, a further rush of visitors came in.

Bella exchanged a few more words with his sister and was then forced to greet the newcomers. Two maids served the refreshments and by anyone's standards this had to be a resounding success for Mrs Burgoyne.

After drinking his coffee and eating a plate full of delicious titbits, he thought they must take their leave. It wouldn't do for him to be seen to outstay his welcome.

On their return, his sister squeezed his arm. 'I'm going back when everyone has left so I can get to know her better. There's no need for you to accompany me. I can see why you're so taken with her — not only is she beautiful, she is also intelligent and witty.'

'I'm glad she has your approval, but I'm not sure I wish you to spend time alone with her. You are notoriously indiscreet . . . '

'Fiddlesticks to that! I shall tell her whatever she wants to know about the family and in so doing will discover what we want to know about her. I suppose tomorrow we must be at home and entertain the square and anyone else who cares to call.'

A hackney carriage drew up outside their dwelling. 'Tarnation take it — it's Mrs Featherstone and I wanted us both to be there when she arrived.'

'Are they so short of funds that they don't have a carriage in Town?'

'I'm certain they are wealthy. Featherstone told me his aunt is somewhat eccentric so that must be the explanation for her extraordinary mode of transport.'

They took the shortcut this time and arrived, somewhat breathless, just as the redoubtable lady emerged from the vehicle.

'There was no need to sprint across the gardens in order to greet me, my lord, lady. I've arrived earlier than anticipated as I decided to travel under my own volition and not wait around until the family carriage was available.'

'Welcome, ma'am, we are delighted to have you with us.' Two footmen were now staggering under the weight of her trunk and, seeing his surprise, she laughed.

'It's books, my boy, I cannot travel without them. The second trunk contains my personal belongings.'

He offered his arm and she took it. 'We are dining at home tonight and we do not change for dinner when there are no guests.'

'I'm glad to hear it, I cannot abide being obliged to forever change my garments.'

Emily glanced at him and raised an eyebrow. He knew exactly what she meant. How could Mrs Featherstone act as sponsor and guide to his sister when she ignored the rules of etiquette herself?

'The housekeeper is here to conduct you to your rooms, ma'am, but we hope you will come down to the drawing room so we may discuss what we're hoping you can do for Emily.'

The sprightly lady with her wildly curling grey hair and extraordinary bonnet looked from one to the other in puzzlement. Simon understood at once he had been gulled by his friend into taking her. Mrs Featherstone was obviously an unwanted relative the family had been eager to move on somewhere.

'Do? I don't understand.'

Emily stepped in immediately. 'I'm hoping you can accompany me to the smaller parties so that my brother isn't obliged to. I can't go on my own and we have no one else in the family who can act as my chaperone.'

'I see, for an appalling moment I thought you expected me to be a conduit to high society or something equally ridiculous. I could, of course, introduce you to a large variety of military gentlemen but I don't suppose that would be of any use to you.'

'No, ma'am, I can't imagine myself following the drum as you did all your married life. However, it would certainly add colour to my ball if I can have a dozen officers in their best regimentals attending.'

'Then I shall draw up a list and you can select from it. Now the war is ended, many of them are kicking their heels at Horse Guards on half pay, hoping for another posting.'

Their guest followed the housekeeper

and they could hear her chatting happily about the neighbourhood as they went. He beckoned his sister into the drawing room and closed the doors behind them.

'We can hardly ask her to leave; it's not her fault she isn't who we thought she was. I did wonder why Featherstone didn't allow me to talk to her for more than a moment or two. I'm not usually so easily taken in.'

'I like her, Simon, and even if she isn't as well connected as we thought, I meant what I said about having officers here.'

'I hate to state the obvious, my love, but she cannot go out in public dressed so bizarrely. There should be time to have your seamstress make her a new wardrobe . . . '

'We cannot afford to do that and it would be unkind to suggest we find her appearance in any way unacceptable.'

He shrugged and admitted defeat. 'I hardly think it matters as I've already made my choice and you're not serious about seeking a husband. Mrs Feather-stone will be a welcome addition to our small family and I'm certain that Annabel will enjoy her company too.'

'And once our fortunes are restored I'll not only be the daughter of an earl but an heiress too. Eligible bachelors will be fighting for my hand.'

'This is no laughing matter, my girl; marriage is a serious business and cannot be entered into lightly. As you still have two years to go before you reach your majority, I can ensure you don't make the wrong choice.'

'Marrying for expedience might be all very well for you, but I intend to fall hopelessly in love before I am wed.'

'Romantic love is a myth, there's no such thing.' He had been about to explain that desire and lust were what drove poets to write sonnets and couples to elope but thought this would be a highly unsuitable topic for an unmar-ried young lady.

'I disagree. I know that marriage has been a disaster in this family for two generations but that doesn't mean we cannot break the mould. Spending the rest of your life with another person not related to you is a daunting prospect. I just think it would make life so much easier for both partners if they are in love with each other.'

'You read too many novels, sister, and your head is filled with nonsense. A sound marriage is based on liking, respect and compatible interests. A different sort of love will inevitably follow, but this will be akin to affection.'

Their conversation was brought to an abrupt close as Mrs Featherstone strode in. His eyes widened when he realised she was wearing a divided skirt and riding boots topped by a blouse cut on masculine lines. At least she wasn't wearing a neckcloth.

'I know what you're thinking, young man: that you can't possibly go into Society with someone dressed as I am. This is the garb I'm most comfortable in; it's what I wore throughout my travels with my dearest husband. I can assure you I'm not so eccentric that I intend to escort you in anything but an unremarkable and elegant silk evening gown.'

'Exactly so, Mrs Featherstone. You can dress as you wish within these walls, and when we return to the country you'll be free to behave exactly as you want.'

He saw tears in her eyes as she took her seat. 'I didn't expect you to make me a permanent member of your family, but I'm overwhelmed by your generosity.' She looked from one to the other, her expression sad. 'We were not blessed with children of our own; my whole life was his regiment. I have sufficient funds to buy myself a small estate but cannot bear the thought of being on my own. I'm used to having people around me — of being of use to those I live with.'

'Then I shan't feel the slightest twinge of guilt when, at some point in the future, we might wish to ask you to leave.' He said this with a straight face and waited to see if she understood he was teasing her.

'Well said, my lord. If I find you and your sister unpleasant company, then it will be *I* that leaves without a second thought.'

# 6

The last caller departed at exactly one quarter of an hour past three o'clock and Bella was relieved to see them go. 'Mama, that was exhausting. Do we have to repeat this process or can we hide in future if anyone comes to the door?'

'Tomorrow it will be our turn to visit those who visited us — that's if they are at home. I cannot credit how many came and I put it down entirely to the good offices of Lord Sawsbury and Lady Emily.'

'I think you might be right, and I have arranged for Lady Emily to come here shortly. We shall go up to my apartment to get to know each other better. She is much more the sort of person I should like to be friends with than Lady Danbury's daughters.'

'That's as may be, my love, but as Lady Danbury has kindly offered to sponsor you, and has obtained all those

103

invitations for us, you cannot ignore them. They might be empty-headed but they are sweet-natured girls and have no malice in them.'

'We are to dine with them tomorrow but I've no plans to meet up with them before that.'

A short time later Lady Emily was announced, and she ran to meet her eagerly. 'Thank you for coming; I could have offered to come to you but that seemed presumptuous.'

'I have so much to ask you and something most amusing to tell you.'

When she heard about Mrs Feather-stone, Bella laughed. 'Papa employed a dreadful woman to be my sponsor but I loathed her immediately and now Lady Danbury is happy to introduce me. I have no wish to go to Almack's, so don't intend to apply for vouchers that would be refused anyway. Do you go there?'

'Unfortunately, my brother has already obtained the necessary tickets. However, I think it quite possible we won't actually go, as I can't see him parading in knee breeches and silk stockings and they won't let him in unless he is so dressed.'

'I imagine he's told you that he intends to marry me. I'm not sure that I shall accept him when he does make me an offer.'

'Why is that? Even biased as I am, I know him to be a handsome man. He is kind, intelligent and his pedigree is impeccable — the only thing he lacks is money.'

Bella immediately stiffened, thinking her companion was implying that if he had money he would not even be considering marrying someone like her.

'No, don't poker up at me. He's not prejudiced against those not of our class like many are. He judges people by their behaviour, not their birth.'

'That may be so, but we both know he would not be looking in my direction if he didn't need my father's wealth to improve his own finances.'

'I must contradict you, Bella, as from the moment you walked into his arms yesterday he was intrigued enough to make enquiries about your identity.'

'Tell me a little about him: what sort of man is he? If he is to pursue me then I wish to know whether I should be running in the opposite direction.'

They were now settled together comfortably in front of the fire in her sitting room, and for some reason she felt completely comfortable with this new friend despite the disparity of background.

'He is six years my senior, which makes him five and twenty. He is an exemplary brother, an excellent land-lord and is liked by all who know him well. However, he is determined to marry for pragmatic reasons and has no time for romantic love. He believes that such strong emotions soon fade and cause harm to both parties in the process.'

'Then he has chosen me because I am an heiress.'

'That was paramount, of course, but the fact that you are so lovely, intelligent and amusing company made his decision easy. Another thing he was quite clear on was that he needs to admire and enjoy the company of whoever he marries and would not look at any young lady who was not as intelligent as himself.'

As this was exactly what she herself had thought until yesterday, Bella was at a loss to know how to reply. 'I'm in no hurry to be married; it's my parents' desire that I marry into the aristocracy. I know that I wish to have children to love, a husband I respect and most importantly he must be a gentleman who accepts my parents as they are.'

'Then as far as I can see, you are ideally suited. We've talked quite long enough about my brother; I wish to know if you are to dine at the Danbury's in Hanover Square tomorrow.'

'We are indeed. I'm delighted that you'll be there too. Do you think there will be dancing?'

'I imagine so. I cannot see any reason why not. In my experience the carpet is usually rolled up in the drawing room and so long as someone is prepared to play, there will be a set or two.'

'To be honest, dancing is the only reason I agreed to come to London. I've perfected all the country dances and even the waltz and have not yet had the opportunity to show off my skills.'

'Then where better to do so than at a small, private party and not in a grand ballroom where you will be on display to so many more critical eyes?' Her friend smiled. 'Although I think it might be wise not to waltz, as that's considered a very daring dance and not suitable for debutantes.'

'In which case I expect we'll both be waltzing tomorrow night, if one is playing.'

Emily's eyes were alight with mischief; Bella knew she had found a friend whatever transpired between herself and Lord Sawsbury.

'I forgot to ask: what is your brother's given name?'

'Simon. He much prefers to be

addressed informally by his friends and family. We don't stand on ceremony — in fact I abhor the fussy rules that govern Society.'

Emily departed soon afterwards. Bella was delighted with the visit and couldn't wait to share what she had learned with her parents. As they didn't change for dinner, she did no more than check her hair was neat, and her gown uncreased, before joining them in the small drawing room.

Her mother looked up with a smile. 'We have received another half-dozen invitations, my love. I cannot understand why these have been sent out so early. I believe that many of these families are not yet in Town, as the Season does not really start until April.'

'Where is Papa? He's usually here before me.'

'It's most unfortunate — he has been called away. We shall dine in the breakfast parlour tonight as there are only the two of us.'

'No doubt some drama relating to his

ships. At least he doesn't have far to go when called to the docks.'

'I don't think it was relating to his business. He was still with Lord Danbury when the letter came and they both departed in a hurry.'

'How very mysterious! Don't look so worried, Mama, I'm sure it's nothing untoward. I can't imagine what has happened that required the urgent attention of both Papa and his lordship.'

'We shan't talk about it anymore. Tell me at once about your visit with Lady Emily.'

★  ★  ★

Simon listened to his sister, and by the end of her recital of the conversation she had had with Bella, nothing had changed his mind about his choice of bride.

'I shall court her, and persuade her that I am in love with her, if that is what it requires to obtain her consent.'

'That would be most unfair, brother.

I'll not stand by and let you deceive her. I consider her a friend already.'

Their conversation was interrupted by the tardy arrival of the new member of their small family. Simon greeted Mrs Featherstone warmly, as did his sister. The guest was dressed in an unremarkable evening gown of dark blue silk. Her wild hair had been restrained and her appearance was perfectly respectable.

'I apologise for keeping you waiting. As I don't have a dresser I find it took me longer than anticipated to improve my appearance.' She gestured to her smart gown. 'I was obliged to wear something of this sort when we attended functions, but it's so long since I did that I quite forgot what was involved.'

'The lack of a personal maid will be rectified immediately. There's a suitable person already employed here who will be ideal as she's older and more experienced than the other girls we employ.' Emily had been running the house this past year so knew more about domestic matters than he did.

'My dear, I did not complain in order to obtain a servant for myself. However, it will be the height of luxury to have someone take care of me and I thank you for your kind gesture.'

Over dinner they conversed freely, at ease in each other's company. Mrs Featherstone had a plethora of interesting anecdotes about her time on the Peninsula to entertain them and, by the end of the evening, he was well-satisfied with the arrangement.

He left his sister to escort her to the drawing room, where he promised to join them shortly. He had much to think about and most of it was on the subject of the young lady who had caught his interest. His determination to win her hand was not entirely because she was everything he wanted in a wife, but also because if he couldn't persuade her then he would then have to prance about Town doing the pretty until he found someone else. He wasn't keen to do that.

When he wandered through, he found the two ladies deep in conversation. His sister looked up and beckoned him over. 'Aunt Jemima has shown me the list of military gentlemen she thinks might well be in London at the moment and I must say I'm most impressed.' She waved the paper at him and he strolled across and took it.

As he scanned the names, his eyes widened. All of them were high-ranking officers and many of them were titled. 'Are all these officers without wives?'

'Good heavens, my boy, of course not. You will see that there is an asterisk against some of the names, to signify the unmarried gentlemen. Emily suggests I invite all of them as well as their wives and adult children if they have any. Do you find that acceptable?'

'We can accommodate a hundred couples easily, but will have to employ temporary staff if so many intend to come to your ball, sister.'

'I've invited barely half that number as I didn't have the names of any more than that. I can imagine the excitement when so many handsome officers stride in. There's nothing like a gentleman in full dress uniform to excite the heart of a young lady.'

Mrs Featherstone — he couldn't bring himself to address her more informally — reclaimed the list and stood up. 'I bid you good evening, sir, and thank you for a most enjoyable time. Emily, I'll write these invitations immediately so they can be sent first thing in the morning. I've the direction of most of them; for those I haven't, the cards can go to Horse Guards as there's ample time for them to be forwarded.'

He nodded politely but his sister jumped to her feet and embraced their guest. When they were alone he asked what her plans were for the following day.

'I'm riding with Aunt Jemima in Green Park. Can you believe that Bella needs to purchase a suitable mount for herself and intends to go personally to Tattersalls in order to select one?'

114

'I hope you told her this wasn't somewhere a young lady should go under any circumstances.'

'I did, of course, but even after so short an acquaintance I'm quite certain she will ignore my advice and go there anyway.'

'Then I must speak to Mr Burgoyne first thing tomorrow morning and make sure that he puts a stop to it. That young lady is given far too much licence and will get into difficulties that even I will not be able to put right for her.'

'You can hardly expect him to be up and receiving before breakfast and that is when she intends to leave.'

'Then I'll be waiting outside her house in order to prevent her departure.'

'This whole problem would be solved if you were to offer to buy her a suitable mount. It would be interesting to see if she trusted your judgement on such a matter.'

'Then that's what I'll do. Perhaps she could come with me in a closed carriage and wait out of sight whilst I inspect what's on offer. I can have a groom parade the horses for her and then I'll bid for whichever animal she prefers.'

★ ★ ★

He was up and ready to leave at first light. His carriage was outside and he'd been assured by his valet that Bella had not as yet set off. The sale itself did not start until later, but the best animals were often sold privately before the auction, so it made sense to be there early.

The air was crisp and cold; there'd been a frost overnight which was hardly surprising at the end of March. His caped greatcoat was enough for him, and Bella would be warm inside his carriage as there were hot bricks and furs waiting for her.

The coachman had instructions to bring the carriage to the archway that led to the stables at the rear of the houses where she resided, and then to wait there for further orders. Simon walked through the gardens to join his carriage. After a quarter of an hour he decided his horses had been standing long enough and told the driver to take them around the square. He went in search of the missing girl and was unsurprised to discover from a nervous groom that the girl had seen his carriage waiting and left via the tradesmen's route.

This was an unmitigated disaster. If she attempted to purchase a horse in person then he could not in all conscience contemplate a union between them. He didn't consider himself a narrow-minded fellow, but a line must be drawn and if he was unable to stop her then she would be lost to him.

★   ★   ★

Bella immediately regretted dashing off so precipitously in order to avoid Sawsbury's interference. In fact, the only way she could have succeeded in her wish to buy herself a suitable horse was with his help. She must have bats in the attic to think she could visit Tattersalls, which was a gentleman's domain: a sporting club, as well as a place where thoroughbreds were sold.

She banged on the roof of the carriage and it rocked to a halt. She remained out of sight on the squabs until the under-coachman climbed down and opened the door.

'I've changed my mind. Turn around as soon as you may and take me home.'

The look of relief on his face was almost comical. 'We can't turn here, miss, but if we continue we'll be on the main thoroughfare and there'll be a square we can use.'

They'd not been travelling long when the carriage halted a second time. There were loud footsteps outside and the door was flung open.

'What the devil do you think you're doing, young lady? You cannot go to Tattersalls. I'll not allow it.' Sawsbury filled the doorway and his displeasure turned her regret at her preposterous actions to anger.

'What I do is not your concern, my lord. Kindly remove yourself from my carriage and allow me to proceed.'

He didn't move and without thinking of the consequences she leaned forward and pushed him in the chest. He vanished and she slammed the door. The coachmen didn't need telling to whip up the horses and take her away from retribution.

At any moment she expected the carriage to be stopped and for him to jump in beside her. She was trembling from head to foot when she returned to the comparative safety of the stables.

Not waiting for the steps to be let down, she jumped out and raced inside and didn't stop running until she was safely in her apartment. Her ears still burned from the appalling language she'd heard as Sawsbury had fallen heavily on his backside in the road.

She prayed that his ignominy had not been witnessed, that it was so early no one had been around. If he called, she would have no option but to go down unless she could think of a reason why she couldn't.

Her maid was hovering anxiously, waiting for instructions. 'I'm not feeling well, which is why I returned. I shall retire and don't wish to be disturbed for any reason.'

Once she was safely behind the curtains of her bed, her pulse returned to normal and she could breathe again. What had possessed her to push him over? She had no respect for anyone, male or female, who used violence and aggression to make their point.

With a sigh of resignation, she scrambled out of bed. Being here was a coward's way and she was no coward. Her maid had the sense not to comment about her mistress wishing to get dressed again immediately.

'Find something plain: no frills or bows, high-necked and long sleeves. Do I have such a garment?'

'You do, miss. It won't take me but a minute to find it.'

Scarcely half an hour after her retreat,

she was downstairs and waiting for the inevitable confrontation. Although she didn't know him well, she was certain he wasn't a gentleman who would allow such behaviour to go unremarked.

She wandered disconsolately up and down the drawing room, listening to the loud tick of the tall-case clock that stood against one wall. The hands crawled round. How could it only be a quarter past seven? Her parents were not early risers — indeed, she wasn't even sure that her papa had actually returned last night.

After an hour, she understood she wasn't to be taken to task directly. This was far worse than receiving a bear-garden jaw immediately. Her stomach roiled and she wished with all her heart that she'd not behaved so badly, that she'd stayed long enough to see if he had been hurt by his fall.

# 7

Simon was back on his feet in one fluid motion, unhurt apart from his dignity. The carriage was already out of reach but to his astonishment it had apparently abandoned the under-coachman. The young man bowed, almost bent double.

'My lord, begging your pardon for speaking to you.' He stopped and chewed his lip.

'Well, out with it, man. You must have had something damned urgent to tell me if you let the coach go on without you.'

'We was turning round when you stopped us, my lord. Miss Burgoyne changed her mind and we was going home again.'

'Thank you for remaining behind in order to tell me that. Now, you can do me another favour. What's your name, by the way?'

'Billy Jones, my lord.'

'Right, Billy. Have you been with the family long?'

'Since I were a nipper.'

'Excellent. Then you will know exactly the sort of horse Miss Burgoyne would like.' The young man began to get his drift and his expression changed and he beamed. 'Jump on the back, there's no room on the box. You're going to help me buy a horse for your mistress.'

It was a short journey to Hyde Park Corner, where Tattersalls was situated behind the Lanesborough Hotel. Simon's coachman could walk the horses in the park until he returned. With Billy beside him, he walked from stall to stall, pleased there were not many others looking to make an early purchase.

'Here, my lord; I reckon this chestnut would suit Miss Burgoyne perfectly.'

Simon agreed with the choice as soon as he set eyes on the handsome gelding. The animal's coat was the same shade as her hair. They would look spectacular together. On enquiring, he was told this horse went side-saddle as well as any other and would also go in harness if required.

After closely examining the animal, he was satisfied Rufus was in perfect condition. 'He's got no vices, my lord, and although he might be considered a tad large for a lady, she'll come to no harm with him.' The young gentleman who owned the horse obviously thought the world of him.

'Why are you parting with Rufus?'

'Debts to pay, my lord, and my father refuses to cough up the flimsies this time.'

A significant sum changed hands and Simon was delighted with his purchase. 'Billy, you can lead him home.'

The young man was already the best of friends with the gelding. 'He's perfect: sweet-natured and intelligent. The mistress will love him.'

As these words were spoken, Simon realised that by buying a horse for Bella he'd made his intentions obvious. Servants gossiped and news of the purchase would be all over the square by this evening. God's teeth! There would be sniggers and nods directed at Bella and himself when they went to dine at the Danbury's tonight. He had the bill of sale in his hand.

'Here, make sure that Mr Burgoyne receives this on your return. He will be relieved that I was able to step in in time and make the purchase for her. Lady Emily was most insistent that I did so.'

'Yes, my lord. We wasn't happy at all about bringing her here, but the young mistress saw sense in the end.'

He tossed the man a coin which was more than ample recompense for walking a mile or two back to Grosvenor Square.

\* \* \*

After breakfasting, he checked his appearance and intended to stroll across to see how his purchase had been received. His sister and Mrs Featherstone were going to ride later, in either Green Park or Hyde Park, but they would take two grooms with them so would be in no danger of offending anyone.

The biggest expense in his household were his horses — one cost more than a servant to keep. When his father had died last year, he really should have sold some of them, but they were his pride and joy; he'd sold an estate in Herefordshire, once owned by his grandmother, instead. Bringing so many horses with him would also keep up the impression that the family was not about to go bankrupt.

He was halfway across the hall when Bella erupted from the corridor that led to the side entrance and skidded to a halt beside him. 'Lord Sawsbury, I cannot thank you enough for Rufus. He's exactly what I would have bought myself.'

Her eyes were shining, her glorious hair escaping from its pins and she had never looked more beautiful. He was about to sweep her into his arms and kiss her when sanity returned.

'Come with me. I need to talk to you in private.'

'No, you can ring a peal over me here. I deserve to be humiliated for my appalling behaviour. I cannot understand why you did something so wonderful for me after I'd pushed you over.'

He put his arm firmly around her shoulders and guided her through the house and into the library where they could converse without being overheard. He was horrified to feel tremors running through her. Was he really so frightening that such a courageous young lady would tremble at the thought of his anger?

He left the door wide open but checked there were no lurking footmen, then turned her round and took her hands. 'Sweetheart, am I so formidable that you are fearful of being alone with me? I promise you I'll never do anything to harm you.'

'I'm sorry, I'm not normally so faint-hearted. For some inexplicable reason I don't wish to be in your bad books.' She managed a hesitant smile.

'I was incensed when you shoved me over, but only for a moment. I'm glad you like Rufus but I now owe you an apology. Sit down, I'll explain why.'

She flopped onto the nearest chair as if her legs would no longer hold her upright. 'I think I can guess what you're going to say. The fact that Lord Sawsbury bought Miss Burgoyne a thoroughbred will be the main topic of conversation everywhere in the square by this evening. Even though you gave the bill to my father so he can reimburse you, the damage is done.'

Without allowing her a chance to protest, he dropped to one knee. 'Miss Burgoyne, will you do me the inestimable honour of becoming my wife? Please make me the happiest of men.'

'If I thought for one moment that you'd orchestrated this disaster in order to trick me into marrying you, I should refuse, however dire the consequences.' Her expression was sad — hardly the reaction one would hope when having made an offer.

'Then you're saying yes?' He smiled, but it wasn't very convincing. 'Can I get up now and stop making a cake of myself?'

'You can; I accept your kind offer. However, I believe you should have spoken to my papa first. I wonder how many other rules we're going to break over the next few weeks.'

He grabbed the nearest chair and moved it closer to her. 'I'll accompany you when you return home and speak to him then. I think we should announce our betrothal tonight and put a stop to any possible gossip.'

'Very well, but I don't want anyone thinking it's anything but an arrangement that suits us both. We have only known each other for two days so how could it be anything else?'

Her colour had returned and she looked more like herself now. 'Why don't we take your new mount out to Rotten Row? I'd like to see how he goes with you. I assume you're an expert rider.'

She was already on her feet, her eyes alight with excitement. 'I should like that above anything. I can be changed and ready in half an hour. Speak to Papa when we return.'

'Emily and Mrs Featherstone are riding this morning and have yet to come down, so we can go out together.'

\* \* \*

'I believe that I can call you Simon now we're to be wed.'

His eyes flashed, and before she could escape, she found herself in his arms. 'And I believe that I can now do this without fear of scandal.'

He tilted her chin and pressed his lips against hers. She'd expected to find this experience somewhat unpleasant, but to her surprise it was the reverse. A delicious tingle travelled from her mouth to a most unexpected region of her anatomy.

She was released just when she had been enjoying her first kiss. He was looking at her quizzically and she smiled.

'That was quite pleasant, I look forward to doing it again.'

His laughter followed her as she ran through the house, eager to get back and change into her habit. She dashed inside her own residence and told the footman who had opened the door for her to send word to the stables that Rufus should be saddled.

The house was still quiet. How could so much have happened and it was still only a little after eight o'clock?

* * *

She settled herself into the saddle. The gelding looked round and nudged her knee as if to tell her she would be safe with him.

'Good boy. I'm certain we are going to be the best of friends.' She told the groom that he would not be wanted, as she would be accompanied by the Sawsburys.

On emerging through the arch, she was met by her husband-to-be astride a magnificent black stallion, and her future sister and another lady, presumably Mrs Featherstone, also mounted on handsome animals.

'Bella, allow me to introduce you to the newest member of our family. She is to be my adopted aunt, Aunt Jemima.'

'I'm delighted to make your acquaintance, ma'am.'

'That horse of yours, my dear, exactly matches your hair. You will turn every head in the park.'

Simon guided his stallion so he was next to her. 'Do you like him?'

'I love him. He's a gentle giant and I can't wait to see how fast he can go.'

'You cannot gallop in the park, Bella. It's not safe with so many other riders around,' Emily told her.

'Then I must bring him there at dawn tomorrow. I shall content myself with a collected canter today.'

As they were moving towards the far end of the square, a carriage pulled up outside her house and her father got out. He hurried inside, head bowed, and a sick dread settled over her.

'I apologise, Simon, Emily, Mrs Featherstone, but my ride will have to wait. I must go back. I fear something catastrophic has occurred to have kept my father out all night.'

He leaned over and took the bit of her horse, preventing her from turning. 'No, sweetheart. Whatever it is, it's better that you let him converse to your mama first. A brisk canter around the park will do us all good. Remember, I'm coming to see him after breakfast.'

Her pleasure in the excursion had gone, but he was right. Rushing back would do nobody any good. Rufus proved as willing and obedient to the bit as any horse she'd ever ridden. Soon she was enjoying the ride. After they had cantered around the park she was happy to be introduced to a dozen or more members of the *ton*. Mrs Featherstone was apparently well thought of and knew more people than Simon. It wasn't until she was turning into Grosvenor Street that her earlier anxiety returned.

'I don't think this morning is the best time for you to ask for my hand . . . ' Unfortunately, Emily overheard this remark even though Bella had spoken quietly.

'Have you come to an arrangement so soon? I'm delighted, of course, but somewhat surprised by the speed with which you've come to this decision.'

Simon dropped back to explain their reasoning, which allowed her to increase her speed to a trot and leave them behind. A groom was waiting to take her horse. She didn't need handing down as she was quite capable of dropping to the ground without mishap, despite the fact Rufus was over sixteen hands high.

On arriving inside, she went at once to look for her parents, even though she was still in her habit. She tried the breakfast parlour; the footmen were just putting out the food, but they were not yet down.

It was unheard of for her to intrude into their private quarters, but she was too worried to bother about that today.

When she approached their shared sitting room, she could hear voices. She tapped but didn't wait to be invited in. She pushed open the door and put her head around it.

'May I come in? Tell me if I'm *de trop*.'

Her father had changed his raiment and was his usual elegant self, however her mama was still in her nightwear and looked as if she hadn't slept at all last night.

'Come in, Annabel. We've grave matters to discuss and they concern you too.'

She joined her mother on the daybed and waited for Papa to explain.

'Lord Danbury invested heavily in my last fleet and he heard yesterday that my ships are lost. They were caught in a typhoon somewhere in the Far East and all sank. As far as we know there were no survivors.'

'Are we ruined?'

'No, but Lord Danbury is. He borrowed heavily against the profits he would have made if our ships had sailed safely back to port. I've done what I can to help him and his family but they will have to leave Town as they can no longer afford the expense.'

'And what I have to tell you will make things easier. Lord Sawsbury and I have come to an arrangement. He made me an offer and I accepted — he will be coming to speak to you shortly.'

Her mother wiped her eyes. 'Oh, I wish he had not done so. Don't you see he is no longer in a position to marry you?'

'But you said that we're still wealthy . . .'

'That's true, but my money is now tied up and you're no longer the heiress able to save Sawsbury's family. I'll tell him that you release him from his promise so he can look elsewhere. We too are going to return home.'

'But this house is rented until the end of June. We will lose money rather than save it if we depart early.' For a moment she was too stunned by this revelation to think clearly. Then something occurred to her. 'I don't know exactly how much Simon needs to clear his family's debts — surely there's still some fluidity in our finances to give him some of what you originally intended?'

'From your vehemence am I to assume that you wish to marry Sawsbury after having only known him for a day or two?'

The conversation was interrupted by a footman, come to tell Papa that Simon was downstairs. Her father stood up, his expression serious. 'I shall talk to him, but first you must answer my question.'

'Yes. Yes, I wish to marry him. In fact, I cannot think of another gentleman who would do as well as he.'

'Then I'll explain the situation to him and see if we can come to some arrangement. Don't be disappointed, my dear girl, if he decides he will jump at your offer to release him.'

'There is something I've yet to tell you. He selected my horse for me and paid for it. He will want reimbursing.'

Her father nodded and marched out. He was still a handsome man despite his advancing age and held himself as upright as he had always done. She got her height from him, but her colouring must have come from a distant relative. Her mother had fading brown hair and hazel eyes; he was darker and with brown eyes.

'Don't look so worried, Bella. We will not founder under this storm. Your father is a clever businessman and has substantial interests in manufactories as well as shipping. The problem is that he doesn't have funds available at present as he has transferred as much as he could to Lord Danbury.'

'Are we still to go there for dinner tonight or is that cancelled?'

'I don't know and I doubt it was anything your papa or Lord Danbury discussed during the night. We shall assume it's going ahead unless we receive a note to the contrary.'

★　★　★

Simon took one look at Burgoyne's face and knew he was going to receive unpleasant news. He bowed politely but the gentleman ignored this and waved him to a seat.

'I'll be brief, sir, and then you may depart if you so wish.'

His heart sunk to his boots. Something had occurred that meant he was no longer considered a suitable candidate for Bella's hand. When he'd heard the whole, he had not given up hope entirely.

'I will be frank, my lord, as my daughter seems set on this union if possible. How much do you need to settle your pressing debts and how long would you be prepared to wait for the remainder of the dowry?'

This was plain-speaking indeed. He named the sum and waited to be told this was no longer available. To his astonishment Burgoyne jumped up and slapped him on the back.

'Good God, young man, I thought you wanted four times that amount. I can clear your debts and give you the same again — the remainder will come once I have liquidated some of my assets. You do understand that keeping Danbury and his family afloat is my priority at the moment?'

Simon was speechless. Until that moment he'd had no idea his future father-in-law was so wealthy. 'Then, sir, do I have your permission to become engaged to your daughter?'

'You do, you do, my boy. I can't think why my little girl is so keen to marry you when only yesterday she was decrying the aristocracy. However, in my opinion you're everything I wanted for her. I know you'll make her happy.'

'I shall do my best, sir. I want you to know that I shall consider you and Mrs Burgoyne to be my parents once Bella and I are married. If you wish to make your home with us I should be delighted to accommodate you. There is an excellent and substantial Dower House in the grounds that could be refurbished and restored to make a perfect second home for you.'

His future father-in-law blinked and cleared his throat before answering. 'I bought a vast estate a few years ago and have regretted it ever since. I'll be happy to sell the place and accept your kind offer.'

'This might be an arranged marriage, sir, but I can assure you the moment I set eyes on Bella I wanted to marry her. It was just fortuitous that she also happened to be an heiress.'

'She's an original. I know my wife and I have given her too much leeway, but she's a good girl and there's no malice in her. I'm sure you'll be able to curb her wildness once you're married.'

# 8

'Daughter, I don't appreciate having you in my boudoir smelling of the stables. I suggest you return to your rooms and do something about it.'

'I apologise for coming in here in my dirt, but the circumstances were unusual, you will admit. Do you think Simon will still want to marry me without the vast fortune he was promised?'

'I don't believe the amount of your settlement has ever been mentioned. I hope that your papa will come to some arrangement with him as he seems to be the ideal gentleman.'

Bella hurried back to her apartment and completed her ablutions in record time. 'I'd like something both warm and pretty — I'm sure there's an ensemble in my closet that will suit.'

Once dressed, she paused for a moment to view her appearance in the long glass. Her hair was tidy, the gown was a becoming shade of gold and the spencer that accompanied it was a lighter colour with the trimmings in the same material as the gown.

She paused outside her rooms, not sure if she should return to her parents' apartment or go downstairs to discover her fate. Her heart was pounding, her palms clammy, and she knew at that moment if Simon had walked away she would be devastated.

How could this be? She was a sensible creature, not given to flights of fancy, but here she was halfway to falling in love with a gentleman she scarcely knew. This was quite ridiculous. It was a business arrangement — nothing more.

As she made her way down the stairs, she heard footsteps approaching. She froze and was about to scamper back when Simon arrived in the hall. If he had taken the opportunity to break the engagement, then it would be easier for them both if she wasn't there.

'Bella, don't run away. Nothing has changed between us.'

Her feet moved of their own volition and she all but fell down the stairs and into his waiting arms. He held her close and she could feel his heart beating as heavily as hers. She looked up at him and his smile made her toes curl.

'I'm so pleased you've been able to come to an agreement with my father, otherwise this would have been the shortest betrothal ever.'

'Come, we cannot talk here. Shall we go into the drawing room?'

He kept his arm around her waist and she didn't complain. She was too agitated to sit so suggested they stroll around the room whilst they conversed.

'My debts . . . '

'No, Simon, it's none of my business. All I care about is that you're still prepared to marry me. Are we to have a long engagement? Shall we take a wedding trip? I don't even know where your estate is.'

'I know you don't wish to be involved

with the financial arrangements, Bella, but I wish to be open with you. Your father has generously agreed to settle my debts immediately, as well as transfer more than sufficient funds for our future. Therefore, there's no urgency for us to marry. If you wish to have a long engagement then that is your decision.'

'I should like to enjoy the Season now that I'm here. Perhaps we could marry in June? As we will be spending most days together over the next few months that's more than enough time to get to know each other better.'

'We can make Emily's ball a double celebration. Please can we stop perambulating about the room and take a seat?'

This time she was happy to settle beside him on a comfortable padded sofa. 'Is your sister serious about finding herself a husband this year?'

'No, she's in no hurry to give up her independence. Also, it might be a year or more before I have enough to provide her with a decent portion.'

There was no need for him to elaborate — he was referring to the fact that the remainder of Emily's dowry was dependent on how soon Papa could replace the loss of one of his fleets.

'Now, I'll answer your other questions. My estate is just outside Oxford and the journey takes no more than a day and a half. As to a wedding trip, I haven't given that much thought. Have you ever visited the Lakes or Scotland?'

'I haven't but I should love to do so. Now you have Mrs Featherstone, Emily will not be left alone when we go away.'

When he told her that her parents intended to make their home with them, she flung her arms around him. His reaction was inevitable. Somehow, she found herself on his lap, and, by the time he raised his head, her hair was tumbling around her shoulders and she was quite dizzy with excitement.

'I hope my performance was more than *pleasant* this time,' he said with a wicked smile.

When she recovered her breath and

her composure, she scrambled off his lap and moved a safe distance away. 'Fishing for compliments, my lord?' She shrugged and put her finger on her lips as if considering her answer. 'I would describe it as enjoyable — but I'm certain you shouldn't be taking liberties with my person even though we're now betrothed.'

'I'm certain that you're correct. However, I believe it was you that initiated — '

'That's as may be, sir, but I am a naïve and inexperienced young lady whereas you are a man about town.'

He rose smoothly to his feet but did not approach. 'I am indeed and have taken shameful advantage of you. I give you my word nothing so reprehensible will take place until after the knot is tied and — '

She rudely interrupted him. 'Fiddle-sticks to that! I've no wish to forego such a pleasurable experience until June. Have we settled on the date or a place for our nuptials?' This time she sat on a chair, not a sofa or *chaise longue*, and he folded his long length on a similar chair opposite to her.

'It's the bride's prerogative to make those decisions. However, in the unusual circumstances surrounding our betrothal, your father and I decided the most convenient place for the service would be in the family chapel at my house across the square in the second week of June. That should give you ample time to prepare your bride clothes and — '

For a second time she interrupted him and his eyes flashed a warning. 'I don't require any bride clothes; I've got more gowns in my wardrobe than I'll ever wear.' She was about to apologise, but he spoke first.

'Annabel, I'm not accustomed to being interrupted so frequently. If you and I are not to fall out then I suggest you curb your tongue.'

She was on her feet in an instant. 'How dare you speak to me like that? I'm not a child to be scolded and you are not my father. Until we marry, I'll thank you to keep your opinions on the subject of my behaviour to yourself.'

If she had poked him with a long stick, he could not have looked more startled by her attack. Before he could react, her parents sailed in, looking as if nothing untoward had taken place.

'We hoped we would find you together,' Papa said. 'I've sent the notice of your nuptials to The Times and it should appear in the paper tomorrow. With everything official, you will be able to enjoy the various entertainments without fear of being pursued by hopeful partners.'

★  ★  ★

Burgoyne stared at Simon as he spoke. Did the man think he would renege on his promise when he had the money? By announcing the date of their marriage, even if he'd intended to jilt Bella, he could no longer do so without being taken to court for breach of promise.

Bella's father appeared benign and friendly, but he couldn't possibly have amassed such a fortune without being a formidable businessman. Although he didn't blame him for protecting his daughter and his money, his mistrust left a sour taste in the mouth.

He was a gentleman and a gentleman didn't break his word. Until that moment, he hadn't realised what a gulf there was between himself and his future family. Had he made a catastrophic error of judgement? Allowed his emotions to over-rule his common sense?

Too late to repine — however much he might come to regret it, he would marry Bella in June.

She smiled prettily at him, but he knew this to be false and he wished the past two days had never happened.

'Simon, there are still one or two things we need to discuss in private. Perhaps you would accompany me to the library where we can talk? Pray excuse us, we shall not be long.'

'Run along, my dear. Now that you're betrothed to Sawsbury you are as much his concern as mine.'

Papa's comment didn't sit well with her and her lips thinned. Simon held out his arm and she had no option but to take it or reveal to her parents that she was angry with him.

As soon as they were out of sight, she snatched it back. They were standing in the passageway, halfway between the hall and the library and study. Although there were no servants visible, there could well be a footman lurking somewhere eager to eavesdrop and then repeat whatever he heard in the servants' hall.

She must be as well aware of that as he, but it didn't prevent her speaking her mind. 'As far as I'm concerned, my lord, you can keep my inheritance. I've no intention of marrying you in June or any other time.'

He caught her arm before she could run away and bundled her into the library which was nearest. She was far stronger than he'd anticipated and only the fact that she didn't wish to draw attention to their struggle allowed him to succeed.

He closed the door firmly and then leaned against it so she couldn't escape. 'It's too late to change your mind. The announcement will be in the paper and my family needs the money.' He'd not intended to mention the money but he was so incensed he'd spoken without thinking.

She stood a few feet from him and he was looking at a stranger. This situation was entirely his fault and now they were both trapped in a relationship from which there was no escape. His anger was replaced by remorse — sadness that his actions had put them in an untenable position.

Then her face crumpled and tears trickled down her ashen cheeks. Immediately he stepped forward to offer comfort but she shook her head.

'No, my lord, it's too late for that. I thought you were different, a man I might come to love, who would be a good father to our children, but I was sadly mistaken. Your interest in me was driven by lust — for money and not for me.' She wiped her eyes on her sleeve like a child. 'I accept that we cannot break this betrothal but I want you to know you have lost my respect and once you have your heir you will not share my bed.'

She turned her back on him and he could think of nothing to say to improve matters. He prayed that in time she would forgive him and he could prove to her he wasn't the villain she considered him to be. 'Then I'll go. We must appear together in public as if we are content with the arrangement. I'm sure you don't wish to upset your parents and I don't want my sister to know the true state of affairs.'

There was no response and he left her to recover her composure without his intrusion. There was a saying about marrying in haste and repenting at leisure. In their case it was becoming betrothed in haste.

He strode through the house, looking neither right nor left, and wanted to be alone to come to terms with the sad mull he had made of things. If he hadn't manhandled her then he might have been able to smooth things over, convince her being married to him wouldn't be a disaster for either of them. However, mentioning the funds he was being given had made an irrevocable rift between them and he only had himself to blame.

Where could he go? He had no wish to return home to be questioned by his sister. His lawyers — they would be delighted to know that by the end of the day funds would be transferred to his account and all his debts could be paid, including the temporary loan from his bank to pay for the sojourn in Town.

If he passed anyone he knew, he was unaware of it. He kept his head down and avoided making eye contact with any of the pedestrians he passed. His conversation with his lawyer cleared his head. He had come to London to marry an heiress and he'd achieved his aim before the Season had even started, so must consider this a triumph not a disaster.

On reflection, he realised that he would not have found a young lady from his own class willing to marry him, that despite the disparity between his family and hers, on balance he had had the best of the bargain. Bella was still the lovely young lady who had fallen into his arms. In three short days, he had managed to find himself the perfect wife and to permanently alienate her.

★ ★ ★

Bella managed to contain her misery until she heard the door close softly behind her. Then she fled to the far end of the drawing room where she was certain she wouldn't be heard and collapsed into the nearest chair. She sobbed into the skirt of her gown, hoping to muffle the sound.

Three days ago, her life had been straightforward, her plans simple; but now everything was ruined. She cried for a while and then slipped out through the servants' door and ran back to her apartment where she could be private. She was glad her maid was elsewhere and couldn't see her in such distress.

She washed her face, hastily removed her gown and was in the process of searching her closet for something else to wear when Annie arrived at her side.

'Let me find something for you, miss. It's my job to take care of you.'

Bella raised and lowered her arms when instructed but took no interest in the proceedings. She was numb and was having difficulty controlling her emotions.

'There, miss, I'm done. Everyone below stairs is talking about your engagement. I'm ever so pleased for you.'

She was about to snap at the girl for her impudence but that would be unfair. As far as the world was concerned, she'd come to London to find herself an aristocratic husband and she'd done exactly that. Simon was everything she'd hoped for and more. Why was she so unhappy that he'd been honest with her? He'd said he was marrying her for her money

— but after all, wasn't that the whole reason for the arrangement?

The tension in her shoulders relaxed a little. She had come to London to find herself an aristocratic husband, so why was she complaining? Simon had no option but to marry an heiress, so he too had achieved his aim.

The remainder of the day dragged as her mother had gone out on morning calls without her and her father was absent on business matters. No doubt he was in the process of transferring funds to Simon.

Her reverie was disturbed by the unexpected but welcome arrival of Emily. 'I cannot tell you how pleased I am to see you; I've been moping about the place all afternoon. Did your brother tell you what transpired between us?'

'I've not seen him since he went out this morning. Tell me at once why you are so blue-devilled.'

When she had finished her sorry tale, instead of being sympathetic or suitably shocked, her friend laughed. Bella could see nothing amusing about the situation.

'Don't you see? It's quite ridiculous for you both to be upset when you've achieved exactly what you set out to do. Simon has acquired a beautiful and intelligent heiress when he could have been obliged to marry a bracket-faced young lady with no manners at all. You have agreed to marry the handsomest and most eligible gentleman on the marriage mart.'

'When you put it like that, I can see why you find my distress amusing. Indeed, I can't understand why I should be upset apart from the fact that I was so impolite to him.'

'I could knock your heads together for your stupidity. The only reason you've both behaved so badly is because your feelings are involved. I'm certain that you are a fair way into falling in love with each other.'

Bella was about to deny this most vehemently but understood there was some truth in what had been said so bluntly. 'I shall endeavour to put matters right between us tonight. There's been no word from Hanover Square that the Danbury party has been cancelled, so I shall see you there later.'

Her friend departed but still neither of her parents had returned. Morning calls only took place between eleven o'clock and three o'clock and it was already almost an hour past that time. Where was her mama? It would soon be time to change and it was unlike her parent to be absent then. Papa obviously kept his own hours and it wasn't her business to know his whereabouts.

They were to have a tray in their chambers this evening and dinner would not be served downstairs. The carriage would be outside at seven o'clock to convey them to the soirée and she could not go on her own.

She retreated to her sitting room upstairs but left the door wide open so she could hear if either of her missing parents returned. Her evening gown was draped over the bed but she wasn't going to begin her preparation until her mother had returned and explained where she'd been for so long.

The nights were lighter now, but dark had fallen before she heard them returning. How were they together when they'd gone out separately? She scrambled to her feet and her precious book fell unheeded to the floor. She rushed into the passageway to greet them.

'Mama, Papa, I've been most anxious these past two hours. Has something untoward occurred?'

'No, daughter. Come with us to our apartment and we shall explain to you why we've been delayed,' her father said. This was obviously something that could not be discussed in front of staff.

The door was closed firmly behind them and Mama checked in both her own bedchamber and her papa's, to ensure no one was eavesdropping. This was all very mysterious.

'Sit down, Bella. We have much to tell you and none of it is good.' She did as her mother bid and sat, her heart beating heavily and her hands clenched in her lap.

'As you know, I went out to make calls to those who visited us yesterday. I was made to feel decidedly uncomfortable and after the third visit was going to return home but decided to visit Lady Danbury instead.'

'Would you prefer that I continue this sorry tale, my love?'

'No, I'll do it.' Mama dabbed her eyes before she continued. 'Lady Danbury was able to explain why I was no longer welcome in any drawing room. That dreadful woman Papa appointed, and you dismissed, has been spreading the most malicious rumours about you.'

'What has she said?'

Her mother was unable to continue, so her father stepped in. 'Your name has been irredeemably blackened. As far as Society is concerned, the lies of one of their own means more than the truth. I think it best if we abandon our stay and return home.'

'What about my betrothal? He can

hardly marry me now.'

Her father's face was hard. 'He cannot renege on his arrangement. The money has been paid. The deal struck. He has no recourse but to marry you anyway.'

# 9

Simon spent several hours with his lawyers and eventually returned home late. Eventually, he returned home late, with barely enough time to change into his evening clothes before he must escort his sister and Mrs Featherstone to the Danbury event.

No sooner had he stepped into the house than Emily pounced on him. 'It's an absolute disaster — quickly — come into the drawing room so I can tell you.'

When he heard about the scurrilous gossip being spread about his future wife, he was enraged. 'Unconscionable, unbelievable — when I discover who is saying that Bella is impure, I'll ruin them.'

'It's coming from Lady Jones, the person that Bella dismissed. Unfortunately, she has the ears of those most likely to enjoy passing on such things.'

'I'll not have anything untoward said about my future wife. When she's seen on my arm tonight — '

'My lord, pray excuse me for interrupting, but I think it more likely the Burgoyne family will already be packing to be ready to leave at the earliest opportunity,' Mrs Featherstone said politely.

'Then I'm going to see them and make sure that doesn't happen.'

'In which case, my boy, I shall rally the troops. If you can delay your arrival until after eight o'clock I think I can muster a dozen or more to stand by your delightful young lady.'

He was warming to this redoubtable woman and he smiled his thanks. 'Emily, is there anyone you can contact who might be attending this event tonight?'

'I don't know anyone in Town as yet, but will help Aunt Jemima write her letters. Good luck with your visit, as I fear you might be unable to persuade the family to remain.'

The front door swung open before Simon reached the steps. He strode in and the butler pointed upstairs. 'The second door on the right, my lord.'

He bounded up the stairs and knocked but didn't wait to be asked to come in. On opening the door, he'd expected to find Bella curled up in a chair sobbing her heart out. Instead, she was striding back and forth across the carpet, her expression murderous.

'Simon, you must have heard what that viper has done. Papa is determined to force you to marry me but as far as I'm concerned you can cry off and I'll make sure — '

'No, I didn't come here to break the engagement. I've come to tell you that those that matter will know by the end of this evening that what's being said is complete nonsense and the perpetrator will get her comeuppance.'

'It's too late. Once a reputation is gone it can never be recovered.'

'Are you prepared to make a wager on that, sweetheart? I come to tell you to put on your finest gown and accompany me in my carriage as my future wife. I don't want your parents embarrassed and I can't protect all three of you tonight.'

There was a flicker of something he didn't recognise in her expression. 'You do realise that by escorting me, by announcing our betrothal, your family could well be put beyond the pale. I would never forgive myself if that was to happen.'

'I can assure you it won't. This Lady Jones person is only on the fringes of society; she has the ears of the tabbies, but no real influence. Do I have your word that you will be ready to leave by half past seven?'

Her smile was tremulous, and he wanted to kiss away her tears, but now was not the time. 'Oh, I most sincerely apologise for behaving in such a brutish fashion earlier today.'

'And I apologise for what I said.'

He stretched out and brushed her cheek. 'Then everything is put right between us. We shall stand together as a family tonight and emerge triumphant. Forgive me, but I must speak to your father before I depart.'

His meeting with his future father-in-law took longer than he'd anticipated. Several glasses of excellent cognac were imbibed before they shook hands, both well-satisfied with the conversation. He dashed across the square and into his own abode, knowing he barely had time to complete his ablutions and get ready.

\* \* \*

Bella, as advised by Simon, paid particular attention to her appearance and approved Annie's selection of evening gown. It was silk; a dark, duck-egg blue, with scalloped neckline and small puffed sleeves. The only adornment was the embroidery around the neckline, cuffs and hem. The cut was so elegant it needed nothing more.

'Will you be wearing white gloves or the ones made to match your ensemble, miss?'

167

'The blue please, Annie, and the cashmere wrap in turquoise.'

With her evening cloak swirled around her shoulders, she was ready to depart. Her hair was arranged elaborately on the crown of her head and a few stray curls drifted down on either side of her face. Papa had given her a lovely set of turquoise jewellery to complement her gown and the necklace and ear bobs were perfect.

Mama came in to admire her ensemble. 'Keep your head high. You have nothing to be ashamed of and you are the future Countess of Sawsbury. Let no one forget that. I cannot tell you how pleased we are with that young man — even if he wasn't an earl, we should still be delighted that our only child is to marry him.'

'I thought he would wish to disassociate himself immediately after he heard the rumours, but the reverse is true. It's hard to credit that someone we've known so short a time already has so great an influence on our lives.'

'The Almighty must surely have been looking down on you and it was He that pushed you into his arms. Are you content with your future now, Bella? No doubts? No regrets?'

'Despite the fact that our lives have been turned upside down within so few days, I'm happy with my choice. Emily thinks our feelings are involved but that's not the case — as far as I'm concerned. My future husband is everything I wanted but it remains an arrangement, nothing more.'

Her mama embraced her, being careful not to disturb her hair. 'As long as you're happy then it matters not the reasons for your nuptials. This evening might well be extremely unpleasant, my love, and I hope you forgive me for saying that I'm glad I don't have to accompany you.'

'It will be my first foray into high society. Naturally, I'm apprehensive that I'll be given the cut direct by everyone we meet, but with Simon and Emily, as well as Mrs Featherstone, by my side, I'm sure no one will have the temerity to insult me directly.'

As she arrived in the hall, he stepped forward, looking magnificent in his evening black. His eyes gleamed with appreciation when he saw her. 'You look *ravissante*, Bella, a diamond of the first water. I'll be the envy of every gentleman present with you on my arm.'

His compliment failed to calm her nerves. 'Are you quite sure about this? I've a dreadful, sick feeling that my disgrace will — '

He closed the distance between them and pulled her hard against him, ignoring the shocked expression on the butler's face. 'You've done nothing wrong. It's that woman who's to blame for any unpleasantness. I can assure you nobody will dare be anything but polite to you tonight.'

'It's not what they say to my face, Simon, it's what they say behind my back. The whispers that will travel around the room as we pass through it that I'm dreading.'

'Remember this isn't a grand, formal affair, but an intimate gathering of friends and acquaintances. Exactly the kind of event for you to make your first appearance as my betrothed. Inevitably there will be a few who initially believed the tittle-tattle, but they will be in the minority.'

He released her and held out his arm. Willingly, she put hers through it. 'Do you think there will be a waltz? I should dearly like to perform it with you, but perhaps that is too risqué for you, in the circumstances.'

His smile was roguish. 'We might as well be hung for a sheep as a lamb, sweetheart, so if there's a waltz played then I'll lead you out.'

He lifted her into the carriage without allowing her to climb the steps. He kicked them up and then jumped in behind Bella. 'Good evening, ma'am, Emily. I hope you're not dreading this evening as much as I am.'

'Things won't be as bad as you fear. There might be a few sideways glances, but nobody will dare to defy Lord Sawsbury and his friends,' said Mrs Featherstone.

'Well said, ma'am, and I thank you for your able assistance in this matter. I hope they provide a decent supper as I'm sharp-set. I didn't have time to dine tonight.'

'How can you think about food at a time like this? My stomach is roiling — the very thought of food makes me nauseous,' Bella replied.

'My brother has a prodigious appetite, Bella; our parents used to say he had hollow limbs.'

Simon was sitting so close to her she could feel the heat from his thigh pressed against her. She rather liked the comfort it gave her. 'I suppose to become so large a gentleman must have required a great deal of eating.'

The journey to Hanover Square would have taken no more than twenty minutes on foot, but it was more than an hour before their carriage halted outside the house. The flambeaux blazed on either side of the short, paved path that led to the front door.

'Look at that, they have put down a strip of red carpet. Do we have to do the same for my ball?'

'I fear so, it's *de rigeur* at all the most prestigious events of the Season. I intend to take you both to Vauxhall Gardens when the weather is more clement. Have you attended any of the events held there, Mrs Featherstone?'

Two footmen, immaculate in their livery, opened the door with a flourish and pulled down the steps. Mrs Featherstone's reply carried wonderfully well to all those making their way to the front door.

'Vauxhall Gardens? A den of iniquity, a scandalous place, and not somewhere I'd recommend that you take Lady Emily or your future wife.'

'I should love to go, Simon. I believe there are masquerades and concerts as well as fireworks and other exciting things,' Emily said.

'Then no doubt I'll be obliged to

escort the pair of you at some point. I'm sure, ma'am, with you to chaperone, no one can cast aspersions in our direction.'

Emily and Mrs Featherstone were handed out first and then she followed. Simon, again ignoring the steps, jumped down beside her.

'I'm surprised it's still so busy as the time is now well after eight o'clock and the invitation stated seven.'

'I believe this isn't the small, intimate soirée we expected. I think there will be more than fifty couples here.' Emily didn't sound at all perturbed about this so Bella decided she wouldn't let it worry her either.

She immediately detected several sideways glances and sly nods in their direction: an indication that the gossip had arrived ahead of them. Lord and Lady Danbury and their daughters greeted them effusively. They couldn't have made it clearer that they were doing everything they could to negate the rumours.

Simon led them through the press of

people and into the comparative quiet of the dining room, which was not yet set out for supper.

'Excuse me, my lord, I'm going in search of my friends. I think it might be wise to have them around us when we join the throng.' Mrs Featherstone sailed away, leaving the three of them together.

There was a sudden, hideous screeching, as if a cat was being dismembered, it was the string quartet tuning up to play. The awful racket defused the tension and they smiled at each other.

'Devil take it! If that's the quality of the musicians I shudder to think what the food might be like.'

She giggled, not something she often did. 'I'd have thought, my lord, that you might be more concerned about the quality of the wine served.'

'Aunt Jemima is a godsend, Simon. I must make sure I thank your friend if he comes tonight. I honestly believe that with her support we'll come through this ordeal unscathed.'

Bella prayed Emily was correct.

She tugged at his sleeve. 'Good Lord, look at that. There must be half a dozen military gentlemen in their best regimentals marching towards us, plus another four or five accompanied by their wives and daughters. I've never seen anything so splendid.'

They were closely followed by Mrs Featherstone, who he thought he might bring himself to call Aunt Jemima from this moment forward.

'Lord Sawsbury, Lady Emily, Miss Burgoyne; allow me to introduce you to my friends.'

After a lot of bowing, curtsying and shaking of hands, he and Bella were now surrounded by a phalanx of supporters. She was no longer looking so pinched and pale and he began to believe the evening would not be the disaster he'd anticipated.

There were so many of them in their party that they filled one end of the drawing room, forcing others to shuffle up in order to make room for them.

'Isn't this jolly, young man? If no one wishes to speak to us then so be it, we shall have an excellent time amongst ourselves.'

'Aunt Jemima, it was a fortunate day for me when your nephew sent you to us. I'll never forget what you've done for us tonight.'

'I've not had so much fun since Waterloo. There's nothing I like better than organising the troops, both literally and figuratively, you understand.'

Their section of the reception room was so lively that, within a short space of time, hopeful guests were drifting around the edges waiting for an introduction. When Danbury and his wife and daughters eventually joined their guests, they too became part of his group. It could not have been plainer to the remainder of the guests that whatever gossip had been spread it was untrue.

'Sawsbury, can I speak to you for a moment in private? Miss Burgoyne is well-protected and will suffer no insult in your absence.'

Bella heard this request and nodded. 'Yes, do go and speak to Lord Danbury. Do you have any objection if I dance first with somebody else?'

He was about to tell her to wait, but she looked so happy he hadn't the heart to do so. 'As long as it's not the waltz, sweetheart, you can dance with any other gentleman in our party.'

There was no need to say any more, as she understood immediately that it wasn't worth the risk of leaving the protection of the group.

In the relative quiet of Danbury's study, he waited impatiently to hear what was so urgent it couldn't wait until tomorrow.

'I owe you an apology, my lord. Burgoyne has had to come to my rescue a second time and this was to your detriment.'

'Devil take it, sir. You owe me nothing. I can assure you that matters have been concluded to my advantage and I'm just glad that you and your family are still solvent after the loss of the fleet.'

'My dear wife told me of the scurrilous rumours that Lady Jones has been circulating. It was only because of that I decided to continue with this party. Between the excellent offices of Lady Danbury and Mrs Featherstone, I think we can be sanguine that Miss Burgoyne's reputation remains intact.'

Simon was overwhelmed by the kindness of a man he scarcely knew — but then Danbury was doing it for his friend, not for him. 'I can assure you your actions are appreciated. We intend to be married at the end of June and would be honoured if you and your family would return to attend.'

'That is most kind of you, my lord, but this house will no longer be available after this week.'

'We have more than enough room to accommodate you and your daughters in Grosvenor Square, so that will be no obstacle to your attendance. If travel is a problem then I'll send my carriage for you.'

'My estate is a day's drive from here and I wouldn't dream of putting you to the inconvenience. I must retrench, but not so much that I'm obliged to give up my carriage.'

They shook hands and Simon went in search of Bella. Fortunately, the musicians played better than he'd expected and there was a lively country dance being performed in the ballroom. There was no difficulty finding his party, as the bright colours of the officers stood out wonderfully amongst the black of the other gentlemen.

He scanned the couples in the three sets upon the dance floor but could not see her. Then she was beside him.

'You were scowling, Simon. I thought you were not as happy to let me dance with another as you pretended. As you can see, I've waited until you returned. As your punishment, you will dance every dance until supper with me whether you wish to or not.' There was something forced about her smile and it worried him. She was doing her best to appear lively and in good spirits but it didn't fool him for one minute.

'If I trample on your feet a few times, I'm certain you will change your tune.' She smiled weakly but ignored his teasing comment.

'Aunt Jemima has told me that the rule of dancing no more than twice with any gentleman doesn't apply to married or betrothed couples. Therefore, we can stand up together as often as we care to.'

'If it is as I wish then it will not be more than once — but I suppose I must indulge you as this is your first public appearance.'

Her smile slipped and he saw unshed tears. She half-turned so only he could hear her. 'I've not ventured anywhere, and have remained firmly within this circle, but Elizabeth and Sarah Danbury have moved about and there are still some here who appear to believe what they heard.'

'I can't understand why this should be so. We couldn't have made it clearer that they were false rumours put about by a spiteful woman of no account.'

'Sarah said Lady Humphrey is telling everyone you are so desperate to have Papa's money you're prepared to take soiled goods.'

He felt a surge of rage unlike anything he'd ever experienced before. Her eyes widened and he tried to school his features and somehow managed to smile.

'Bella, can you point out this person?'

'Even if I could, I would not do so. There's nothing you can do, Simon. We will keep a brave face on things tonight but then we must accept the damage is done and nothing we say or do will bring back my good name.'

He could have lied to her, told her what she wanted to hear, but if their marriage was to be successful they must be honest with each other. 'I fear you're right, my love, but once we're married and you're the Countess of Sawsbury, things will be different. I know of at least two eminent peers who have married their mistresses and these women are now received in all the best drawing rooms.'

'I wish it were otherwise; I might be naïve but I'm not stupid. The set is coming to an end but I no longer wish to dance. I'd much rather go home.'

'Listen, it's the waltz. We shall dance that together and be damned to the tabbies.'

# 10

To Bella's surprise, instead of being led through the suspicious crowd alone, all the officers paraded around them with suitable partners. Even dear Aunt Jemima was going to waltz in order to support her.

The ballroom floor was empty. A strange hush had fallen and she believed that every eye was upon her. She was walking much closer to Simon than was considered proper, but in the circumstances, she was grateful for his proximity — she doubted her legs would have carried her forward without it.

'Smile, my love, brazen it out. Have you noticed that the Danbury girls are waltzing with two of Aunt Jemima's officers? If they can defy the rules for you then you must be brave.'

His words were enough to stiffen her

spine and force her mouth to curve. The musicians played with gusto and before she had time to protest, she was dancing. This was not a dance she'd practised overmuch and she had feared she would forget the complicated steps, as they involved not only parading side by side but also spinning around the floor with his arm around her waist.

However, the moment she began to dance with him, her reservations vanished, and her smile became genuine. They swirled around the floor and were immediately joined by the other dozen couples in their party. This meant there was no room for anyone else and by the time the last chords were played, a dozen eager young ladies and their partners were waiting on the fringes of the floor for their turn.

'That was quite wonderful, Simon. If it wasn't for the fact that to do so would deprive others of the treat, I would insist we danced again.'

'I've spoken to Danbury and there will be half a dozen waltzes played tonight. This is a family gathering, albeit a rather large one, and the rules of etiquette don't apply so strictly. We shall dance again, but perhaps wait until after supper.'

He led her, again accompanied by their protective barrier of scarlet, blue and gold, around the edge of the ballroom. Although he was smiling and chatting, his eyes were hard, and she swallowed a lump in her throat. Someone had unwisely told him who the perpetrator of this gossip was, and he intended to speak to her.

They halted in front of a portly matron wearing an extraordinary turban with half a dozen wildly waving ostrich feathers attached to it. Her gown, also burgundy, did nothing to disguise her spreading figure.

'Please, Simon, don't confront her.'

He glanced down and smiled. 'Never fear, my love, I'll do nothing to embarrass you further.'

'Lady Humphrey, I am Sawsbury. I believe you have something to say about my future countess. Would you care to repeat it to us?'

The unfortunate lady first turned the same colour as her ensemble and then her cheeks paled. Bella glanced at her future husband and he looked quite different. His arctic stare pinned Lady Humphrey to her chair.

'My lord, I believe I was misinformed. I give you my word I shall ensure that everyone knows the rumour to be untrue.'

'It would have been better, madam, for you not to have spread such vile untruths in the first place. You will not be received anywhere in future. I suggest that you leave immediately.'

The wretched woman rose unsteadily to her feet. 'Perhaps you would be kind enough to convey a message to your friend, Lady Jones?'

The ostrich plumes danced as she nodded vigorously.

'Excellent. I have a long reach and her perfidy will not go unpunished.'

No more was said. The entire

conversation had taken no more than a few moments, but he had, by his few words, possibly changed everything for her.

'You are quite terrifying when you're angry, Simon. I almost felt sorry for that woman.'

'Then do not do so; she and her ilk are the scourge of Society. They thrive on spreading gossip and like nothing better than to see lives ruined by their cruelty. I can assure you by the time I've finished with the pair of them they will rue the day they spread falsehoods about you.'

The remainder of the evening was quite different as the atmosphere had changed and everywhere she looked people nodded and smiled. She danced two more waltzes but declined the invitation to stand up in a country dance.

Supper was plain but plentiful — exactly what they both needed after the excitement earlier. At midnight, the carriages were called for, and she thanked her gallant soldiers and their partners before Simon escorted her back to the carriage.

'We can't depart; Emily and Aunt Jemima are not here.'

'They are staying until the end. I believe that my sister is enjoying having the attention she's getting from those officers. Three of them are unmarried and all perfectly eligible.'

'Perhaps I should have danced with one of them — but then my hair would have clashed horribly with their jackets.'

The interior of the carriage was dark and chilly after the warmth and light of the house. He dropped down beside her on the squabs and immediately his arm was around her waist. He drew her close to his side.

'I enjoyed this evening but I don't think I'll attend any more events, apart from Emily's ball in a few weeks' time.' She sighed and relaxed into his arms. 'Even with you at my side, I really don't think I can face another night like tonight.'

'Then concentrate on visits to the sites, and only accept private invitations. I guarantee there'll be plenty from Aunt Jemima's cohort of military friends. We can also ride and drive in the park every day.'

'You don't mind if we avoid the major events and balls?'

'Mind? I'm delighted that you have no interest in such things. Thank God I now have a companion and chaperone for Emily so I don't have to accompany her everywhere.'

'Her ball is not for another four weeks — I would much rather retire to our estate and not attend anything at all.'

'I have a better suggestion: why don't we all, including your parents, go to my estate? There are bound to be changes you want to make, so it makes sense for you to see the place before we marry. That way, I can get everything in hand.'

'If my mama and papa are to live in your Dower House then they, I'm sure, would prefer to see it before they move.'

The return journey had been much shorter as there was no queue of carriages in front of them. It had rolled to a halt outside her house. 'Thank you for an interesting evening. Hopefully my parents won't have retired yet so I can tell them we're going to Sawsbury. When will we be leaving?'

'I must discuss this with your father. Allow me to assist you from the carriage and then I shall come in and speak to him myself.'

The front door swung open and as they approached, they were bowed in by a footman. 'Forgive me, Simon, but I'm going to retire. I'll leave you to arrange things in my absence.'

She slipped past him and was halfway up the stairs before he could react. Not only had she ruined her own good name, she might very well have caused irreparable damage to Emily. Then she smiled — from what Simon had told her, his sister had not been bothered in the slightest by the unpleasantness, otherwise she too would have wished to leave the party early.

Annie helped her disrobe and then was able to go to her own bed. It didn't seem right that her maid had to stay up so late and still be available at seven o'clock in the morning. In future, Bella decided, she wouldn't ask her to wait up.

With the curtains pulled around the bed, the shutters closed and the fire burning merrily in the grate, she was almost able to forget that her name had been blackened. Simon had said he intended to deal severely with Lady Jones, but in her opinion this pernicious widow was best left alone. Ensuring that she was no longer welcome in the *ton* would be enough to prevent further damage.

She tossed from side to side, her head full of insoluble problems. Why was she so bothered about what had been said when her future husband and his sister appeared to be quite unperturbed? Running away to his country estate might well compound the rumours. On the other hand, if they were not in Town for a spell then no doubt something more salacious would become the topic of conversation behind the fans.

There was nothing she could do about it, as her parents and Simon were at this very moment making arrangements of one sort or another. The weather was good so she would ride Rufus; if they stopped frequently, he could do the journey easily, and so could she.

*　*　*

The next day was spent in a flurry of packing and organisation for their impromptu visit to Sawsbury Hall. Her mother had said Emily and Aunt Jemima had decided to come too, rather than remaining in London on their own.

'Papa, I'm sure you'll have no objection when I tell you that I intend to ride my new horse on this visit.'

'No, my dear, you may do as you please. Your mama and I are going first to our estate so we can decide what items we wish to bring with us. I have instructed my lawyer to put the place on the market and it will be advertised in the next few days.'

'It's a highly desirable place, Papa, even though none of us felt comfortable there. Will you be sorry to see it go?'

'If I recoup what I paid for it then it will go a fair way to restoring the losses I incurred recently. This will mean I can transfer the full amount of your inheritance to his lordship.'

'Are we to travel together, do you know?' Bella carefully avoided commenting on this latest piece of information. She feared if word of this got out the rumour mill might well consider it the only reason that Simon had offered her parents a home on his estate.

When he appeared that afternoon, she immediately mentioned that she intended to ride. 'Papa is quite happy for me to do so. I hope you will not be travelling in your carriage as I'd much prefer to have you beside me.'

'I wasn't intending to travel on

horseback, but will now do so if you're determined to ride rather than travel in comfort in a carriage.' He did not look overjoyed at the prospect. 'I cannot gainsay your father, as he has given you permission, but I can assure you I would not have done so.'

A faint flicker of unease made her wish she'd not begun this small deception. The discussion she'd had with her papa had been deliberately ambiguous and she was certain he'd interpreted her comment as meaning that Rufus would accompany them, not that she would be riding herself.

Hopefully, he would assume that Simon had given his permission and would therefore not question it. If ever it came out, she would get her comeuppance, and the set down she would receive from her future husband would be worse than anything she'd ever had from her devoted parents.

★  ★  ★

Aunt Jemima and Emily took care of the letters of apology to those invitations they'd already accepted. His sister had pointed out that it might seem as if they were running away but as he had no interest in the opinion of society, he ignored her warning.

The entire day was taken up with business matters. They would spend two weeks in the country and then return the week before the ball. Everything was in hand for that event and also for his wedding — the funds he needed to restore his family fortunes were now in his possession and as far as he was concerned, he would be quite happy not to return to London at all.

The servants and baggage set off at dawn the following morning and his carriage with his sister and her companion left immediately after breakfast. With his groom in attendance, he rode round to Bella's house and was surprised, but pleased, to find her mounted and waiting with her own groom at her side.

'Good morning. The more I see of

you on that horse, the more I think he's the perfect match for you.'

'Good morning, my lord, it's an ideal day to ride. Do you like my new habit? No doubt you've noticed that green is my favourite colour.'

'It suits you well. We can travel across country and will meet up for refreshments and to rest the horses at midday. Luncheon has been arranged and there will be a private parlour set aside for you.'

'I'm hoping there will be somewhere we can gallop, as I've yet to see how fast Rufus can go.'

'It would be foolish to push our mounts when we've so far to travel.' Her eyes narrowed and he thought she was about to argue, but she nodded instead.

'That makes perfect sense.'

They clattered through the streets where most of the houses were still quiet; the occupants would not rise until mid-morning at the earliest. There were servants about their business, but little traffic to delay them.

A small terrier dashed out of an alleyway, yapping at the horses' hooves. Rufus shied but she remained steady in the saddle and soon calmed him. Apart from that, their departure from Town was uneventful and soon they were cantering along a country lane enjoying the spring sunshine.

There had been little opportunity for casual conversation but he was enjoying her company and was impressed by her seat. Rufus was the same height as his own horse which, in his opinion, meant he was too large for her. He should not have purchased such a tall animal. Once they were married he would buy her something more suited to a lady and persuade her to abandon the gelding.

They arrived at the Rising Sun ahead of the carriages, but that was only to be expected. The grooms took care of the horses and he escorted Bella into the hostelry.

The landlord bowed. 'Welcome, my

lord, everything is ready for you. Miss Burgoyne, if you would care to follow the maid she will take you to a chamber set aside for your use.'

She smiled and went with such alacrity he thought her need for the facilities urgent. He was taken to a similar chamber where there was hot water and towels left ready for him. He completed his ablutions and strolled downstairs, just as the carriage containing his future in-laws trundled in.

He went outside to greet them. 'Did you have a smooth journey, sir? We arrived only a short while ago ourselves.'

'I must say, my boy, I was somewhat surprised that you wished for my daughter to ride with you. I'd much prefer her to be in the carriage with us.'

'I was under the impression that you had given her your permission. I believe we have been thoroughly deceived, sir. I can assure you that your daughter will complete the remainder of the journey with you.'

On enquiry, he was directed to the chamber she was using. He knocked loudly and then stepped in without waiting for permission. The room was empty. He frowned. How could this be? He would have seen her descending the stairs. He walked to the window and immediately everything was clear. She would have seen him talking to her father and realised the deception had been discovered.

She was wise to absent herself, as he was very certain she would regret her misbehaviour by the time he'd finished talking to her. He could hardly take her to task in public so he guessed she would be in the parlour with her parents, hoping to escape his displeasure.

However, when he walked in, she wasn't there. 'I've yet to locate Bella, has she been in here?'

Mrs Burgoyne replied. 'No, my lord, we've not seen her at all. I expect she's hiding from you in the hope that she will avoid a bear-garden jaw by doing so.'

'Sit down, my boy, and enjoy the delicious repast they have set out for us. If my girl misses her lunch, then that is no more than she deserves in the circumstances.'

Simon hesitated but then decided he would not go in search of her. Having to travel the remainder of the day hungry would indeed be a suitable punishment. There was now no need for him to take her to task.

Emily and Aunt Jemima arrived and joined them in their private parlour for luncheon. He thought that an hour would be long enough to rest the horses as they'd not travelled at speed. 'I'll go in search of my missing bride-to-be when we've eaten. I need to make it clear she's not riding any further.'

*   *   *

Bella knew instantly that her deception had been discovered. Simon's face, which she could see clearly from her vantage point at the window, registered

his annoyance. He would come immediately to find her and stop her riding.

All her life she had been indulged,
allowed to go her own way, but once
she was married to him all this would
come to an end. Until the knot was
tied, she intended to do as she pleased
and not be curbed by his wishes. There
was only one thing she could do and
that was to set out with just her groom
for company; then he would have to
catch up with her in order to stop her
riding Rufus. Of course, she would get
her comeuppance this evening but
would have the remainder of today to
enjoy her freedom.

She found the back stairs and
escaped through them and out into the
stable yard. The horses had had half
an hour to recover and she was certain
they would be ready to go without
detriment to their health. Her groom
was with Rufus and didn't query her
demand that he saddle both horses and
that they leave immediately.

Once they were a mile away from the

inn, she was able to breathe easily again. 'Do you have any notion of where we're going?'

Her groom nodded. 'It ain't that difficult, miss. I know the name of the town and I reckon we'll find it easy enough. I'll just ask for the King's Head when we get there.'

Neither of them mentioned the likelihood of them being overtaken by a very angry gentleman and so she decided to ignore this unpleasant possibility and enjoy riding through the English countryside on her magnificent horse.

Twice they were obliged to stop in order to ask directions, and at one of the inns she was concerned to discover that there was a group of young bucks staying there after having attended a cockfight nearby. She was sure she hadn't been seen, because if she had, one of the gentlemen would have emerged from the taproom to ogle her.

# 11

Simon was enjoying a particularly tasty beef pasty when the landlord sidled in looking most uncomfortable. 'Forgive me, my lord, but your groom wishes to speak to you urgently.'

'Excuse me, sir, ma'am. I'd better see why I'm needed. I fear it might be because one of the horses is lame.'

'I think it more likely your bird has flown, young man,' Aunt Jemima said with a wry smile.

He was outside, hearing the bad news, in seconds. 'There weren't no room for all of us at the same end of the barn, my lord, so we never noticed Miss Burgoyne and her groom had gone until just now.'

'God's teeth! She could well have an hour's start on me. Have our horses in the yard immediately. I must explain to her parents before I set off after her.'

He had no need to go back into the inn as everyone was now outside. 'I apologise for my daughter's behaviour, my lord. She tends to go her own way.'

'I will put a stop to that, sir, you may be very sure. I believe she must have bats in her attic to think riding off with just her groom for company was a sensible thing to do in the circumstances.'

Emily touched his arm. 'Please don't be angry with her, Simon. She's giving up a lot for you and will be well aware this might well be the last time she can do as she pleases.'

'You're right, but I'm angrier with myself for not realising that she'd gone until now. At least when she was riding with me she was protected — now anything could happen.'

'Then I suggest, my lord, that you get after her. I take it you know exactly which direction to follow?'

He bit back a sharp retort. 'Ma'am, I intend to do just that. I think it highly unlikely I'll overtake her before she reaches our overnight stop — but I'll be there shortly after her arrival. I don't want her to be deemed to be unescorted.'

There was no need for him to elaborate, his surrogate aunt understood immediately. He was familiar with the countryside. Bella wasn't, and this gave him the advantage. He could travel as the crow flies whereas she would have to remain on the better-known route in order not to become lost.

He thundered across country, jumping the hedges and ditches with scant regard for his or his mount's safety, determined to reach his destination ahead of her if he could possibly do so. He reined in a mile or so from the town to allow the animal to cool down — it wouldn't do to arrive with his horse hot and blown, as this would give rise to speculation.

As they turned into the toll road on which the King's Head was situated, he saw his quarry just ahead. He pushed his mount into an extended trot and arrived at her side a hundred yards from the inn.

'There you are. I hope you enjoyed your ride.' He'd expected her to look dismayed at his sudden appearance. The reverse was true.

'I'm so pleased to see you, Simon. I was reluctant to enter the yard on my own.' She smiled hopefully at him, but he did not respond. 'I must admit I expected you to catch up with me far sooner than you have.'

His hand tightened on the reins, making his horse toss his head. He took several deep breaths before replying, knowing he had to be careful what he said if he didn't wish to draw attention to themselves. Was it possible she had no idea just how angry he was at her behaviour?

'I think it would be best if we continue this discussion in private. I'm assuming our luggage and staff will be here and our chambers ready, despite the fact that we have arrived somewhat sooner than expected.'

They clattered into the yard and she had dismounted before he had the opportunity to do so himself. Somehow his path was blocked by Rufus and the groom and by the time he'd stepped around she had vanished. He cursed under his breath, knowing he'd been thwarted a second time. She would already be in the safety of her own bedchamber, guarded by her maid.

His own rooms were more than adequate, having a private sitting room attached as well as a dressing room in which his valet could sleep. The only disadvantage for someone of his height was that he had to remember to duck his head on entering any room if he didn't wish to be floored.

He changed his raiment and went in search of refreshments. The carriages wouldn't be here for another three hours and he was determined to speak to his recalcitrant bride before her doting parents arrived. Fortunately for her, he didn't believe in corporal punishment for disobedient young ladies or children. If he did, she might well have reason to hide from him.

After some consideration, he decided he would go to her room and explain exactly why he was so furious with her. He didn't give a damn if her maid repeated what she overheard — it would be part of Bella's punishment for her transgressions.

The landlord had given him the location of her room and he knocked loudly on her door. There were hesitant footsteps on the other side and then it was opened by a terrified maid.

'Miss Burgoyne is unwell, my lord, and is about to retire . . . '

He ignored this falsehood and stepped around the girl. To his horror, Bella was standing in her petticoats. It was impossible to say who was more shocked by his intrusion. He was about to retreat into ignominy when to his surprise she laughed.

'You might as well come in, Simon; it's too late for you to unsee me in my underpinnings.' As she was speaking, she scooped up her dressing robe and hastily pushed her arms into the sleeves and tied the sash.

He ran his finger around his stock, which had become unaccountably tight. 'I apologise for intruding. It's not something I thought I'd be doing on this visit.'

'Are you very angry with me? I know I shouldn't have left on my own — it was a stupid thing to do, especially as neither my groom nor I had any clear idea of the route we should take. Why didn't you overtake me?'

'I didn't realise you had gone until an hour had passed and by then you were too far ahead. Believe me, I did my best.'

She curled up in front of the fire, tucking her feet under her bottom and ensuring not an inch of flesh was visible. He took the seat opposite, not sure how he could make his displeasure plain when his sin was far worse, and she'd forgiven him instantly.

★ ★ ★

Bella had never been more pleased with anything than when he burst into her room and saw her as she was. It gave her the moral advantage and would take the sting out of whatever he had been intending to say to her.

She watched the play of emotions on his face but didn't know him well enough to interpret exactly what he was feeling or what he intended to do. What if he wished to beat her for her disobedience? No sooner was the thought in her head than the words tumbled from her mouth.

'Are you going to beat me?'

He jerked as if she'd stuck him with a hatpin. 'Good God, of course not. Although you must own that you deserve it. What were you thinking of? Isn't your reputation fragile enough without adding fuel to the fire? Don't you realise, you silly girl, that such behaviour could have made it impossible for me to marry you? You would ruin me by doing so; not just me, but Emily as well. Is that what you want?'

'Of course it isn't. If you were not so terrifying I would never have done anything so silly.'

He sat back, folded his arms and fixed her with his steely gaze. 'So, you're now saying that the fault is mine? Was lying by omission to both me and your parents about having permission to ride in the first place also my fault?'

She wriggled uncomfortably. Somehow his reasonable tone was more frightening than if he raised his voice. If she wasn't going to be spanked then why was she so nervous of him?

'I've always done as I please and am well aware that this will stop once I'm married to you. I just wished to do something reckless for the last time before I become a sedate married woman.'

If she had announced she was about to become a devil worshipper he could not have looked more surprised. He sat forward and she couldn't help flinching.

Instantly his expression changed and in two steps he was beside her. He dropped to his haunches and took her hands in his.

'Little one, you must not be afraid of me. I'm not a violent man and don't believe in any sort of physical punishment — not for you or for children. Do you give me your word you'll never do anything like that again?'

She nodded, but for some reason was unable to form a coherent sentence when he was so close to her. Her hands trembled in his and this time it wasn't from fear but anticipation.

He was on his feet and by the door in one smooth movement. 'I'm waiting for your answer, Bella.'

'I'll do my best to behave, Simon, but I can't promise I won't transgress occasionally.'

His voice was gruff when he replied. Was he going down with a head cold? 'There's no need for you to retire, you must be starving having not eaten since first thing this morning.'

Forgetting the reason he'd moved so smartly to the furthest side of the room, she scrambled from the chair and ran over to him. He held up his hands to ward her off but she ignored his gesture and was about to throw herself into his arms.

The outraged gasp from Annie brought her to her senses. 'Are we friends again? I thought you'd ring a peal over me that I'd not recover from for weeks.'

His smile was unnerving. 'Believe me, my love, you'll get your comeuppance once we're married. I'm prepared to bide my time until then.' He turned to go but then turned back. 'I'm more disappointed in your deception than your running away. You will not lie to me again. Do I make myself clear?'

'I didn't lie, I just didn't tell the entire truth which is quite different . . . ' His eyes narrowed and she wished the words unsaid. 'I apologise; you're right to demand I don't deceive you again even on the smallest point.'

He nodded and was halfway through

the door when she couldn't stop herself from speaking unwisely.

'I hope this honesty is reciprocal, my lord — that you intend to be as open and honest with me.'

Her heart almost stopped beating as he froze in the door and turned to face her. There was something implacable about him; she'd touched a nerve and wished the words unsaid.

'I think, Annabel, you will regret that request. There are some things between a husband and wife that are better left unspoken.'

With that cryptic remark, he left her with more questions than answers. Did he have secrets she would prefer not to know about? Or did his comment refer to his opinion of her? Although she had not eaten since first light, her appetite had deserted her.

'Annie, that encounter with Lord Sawsbury was most unpleasant. I'm not feeling at all the thing and intend to retire as planned. I shan't require a supper tray. Once I'm abed you're free for the remainder of the evening.'

Her abigail bobbed and nodded. 'Thank you, miss, I much appreciate your kindness. I'll be in bright and early with your morning chocolate and sweet rolls — that's if they have such a thing at this place.'

'I need you to inform my parents that my indisposition is trivial and merely brought on by overexertion.' She didn't want her mother or Emily coming in to disturb her.

The bed was an old-fashioned tester and with the curtains closed she was cocooned in darkness with only the sound of the fire crackling for company. She was indeed exhausted, both mentally and physically. She had ridden for hours and had never done so before.

It would be a relief to travel in the carriage with her parents tomorrow as this would remove the necessity of talking to Simon or his family. A week ago, when she'd arrived in Town, her plans had been simple. Find herself a compliant aristocrat and marry him.

No emotions, no love involved — just a business arrangement between friends.

Now she was about to be married to the least biddable gentleman in the kingdom and it was entirely her own fault. He was right to castigate her. Right to say that if anyone of note had seen her gallivanting about the countryside with just her groom for company she would be so far beyond the pale even his good name could not save her. She shivered as she recalled the place they had stopped for refreshments and how they had left hurriedly because there were gentlemen from Town already there. Was it possible someone had seen her through a window that she'd not been aware of?

If this were so then her name would be further blackened. She would be unmarriable, he would be honour-bound to return the money to her father — even though she would insist he kept it — and her stupidity would have ruined them all. Tears seeped unbidden from beneath her eyelids and her pillow was sodden before she eventually fell into a restless sleep.

She woke in the night, her mouth dry and her stomach rumbling from the lack of sustenance. Tomorrow she must make sure she ate a substantial breakfast before they set off. The inn was silent — no — that wasn't true. There were no human sounds but there were creaks and groans, the occasional pitter-patter of rodents in the ceiling above her, and foxes called and owls hooted in the darkness.

She was up and dressed when Annie came in at first light with her morning tray. She'd washed in cold water and braided her hair and arranged it in a coronet around her head. This would make wearing a bonnet uncomfortable, but she cared not about such trivialities.

'Miss Burgoyne, you should have rung the bell and I'd have come to attend you. Here are your chocolate and rolls.'

After a few sips, she pushed the drink aside and attempted to eat one of the rolls. These were warm, crisp and tasty but turned to sawdust in her mouth and she couldn't swallow. Whilst her maid was busy repacking her overnight things, she hastily hid the remaining food in her handkerchief to dispose of later. She tipped the chocolate into her chamber pot and then returned to the small table by the window.

'If you have everything you need, miss, then I must go, if the luggage is to arrive ahead of you today.'

Bella wandered disconsolately around the room and then decided to go downstairs and see how her horse had recovered from his exertions the previous day. Her groom would have to lead him, but no doubt he was quite capable of doing so.

She checked Rufus and he appeared pleased to see her. 'Good boy. I'll see you tomorrow, if you're recovered.'

When she emerged from the stables, she heard the sound of running water and decided to investigate. After several false turns, she emerged on the riverbank. There was a narrow path running alongside the fast-flowing stream; it was hardly wide enough to qualify as a river, and she walked along it for a while. There was a solid brick wall that presumably bordered the grounds of the hostelry they were staying in.

For some strange reason, her eyes were blurred, and she felt decidedly strange. She would sit on the wall and recover her equilibrium before making her way back. There had been no one apart from the servants up when she left but she was certain her party would be down for breakfast very soon. She had apologies to make to them as well, before they set off for Sawsbury.

As she approached the wall, her foot slipped on a clump of wet grass and she tumbled forward. There was a searing pain in her head and her world went black.

* * *

When Bella failed to appear for breakfast, Simon was concerned. 'Has anyone seen her this morning?'

No one had, so he abandoned his food and went up to her room. This was empty, and as her maid had departed some time ago, he couldn't enquire from her where she might be. Next, he headed for the stables, and again, no one had seen her there.

He was now seriously worried. One thing he was quite certain of was that Bella wouldn't do anything to upset him after giving her word she would conform in future. He was joined by Mr Burgoyne.

'No sign of her, sir. I think we have to look further afield.'

'Find the grooms, young man, and I'll round up as many men as I can to help with the search.'

Emily rushed up to his side, her face etched with worry. 'Something untoward has taken place, there can be no other reason why she's missing. I'll come with you; we might find her the sooner if we work together.'

After an hour of fruitless searching

and still no sign of her, Simon was becoming desperate. Emily had returned to the inn in the hope that someone else had better news. Then he was hailed by an old man with a dog. 'Over here, sir, the young lady's met with an accident.'

Simon vaulted the wall in front of him and saw her spread-eagled on the grass. For a split second, he thought her deceased. She was so still, so white and there was so much blood. Then he dropped to his knees beside her and felt for her pulse. It was weak but discernible.

He ripped off his stock and then snatched his handkerchief from his inside pocket. He folded this into a pad and pressed it across the gash on her forehead, and then held it in place with the strip of white cotton he'd removed from around his neck.

The old man stood by, muttering to himself. 'Pretty young thing like her shouldn't be a wandering around by herself, mister. She could've died here if I hadn't come along and raised the alarm.'

'I thank you for your assistance. If you would care to come to the King's Head, you'll be recompensed for your trouble.'

He put one arm under her knees and the other around her shoulders, leaned back on his heels and swayed to his feet. There was no time to lose. He raised his voice. 'I've found her, I'm bringing her in. Someone send for the doctor.'

His words carried and immediately there was a response. Burgoyne appeared at a run. 'Follow me, I'll show you the quickest way back.'

It took him ten minutes to return and, in that time, Mrs Burgoyne had things arranged as they should be in the bedchamber. 'Put her on the bed, my lord. Mrs Featherstone and I are experienced in such matters. She has gone to fetch her first aid kit and will be able to put in any sutures without the necessity of fetching the local sawbones.'

He was reluctant to leave her but knew when he was redundant. Burgoyne took his arm and all but dragged him down to the private parlour. 'Sit down, my boy, you're almost as pale as my girl.'

Simon closed his eyes for a moment, unable to comprehend what had transpired. If he had lost her, he would have been bereft. At that moment he understood he'd fallen irrevocably in love with her. This was no longer a business arrangement, as far as he was concerned, but a love match.

The glass was pushed into his hand and he drained it without thought. Cognac scorched his throat and he coughed. 'Now, hot coffee with plenty of sugar is what you need.'

He was beginning to feel better when his sister burst in. 'How dreadful! Do you know what happened? I sent for the doctor but he's away from home delivering twins and not available.'

'Aunt Jemima is taking care of matters for us. The time she spent on the Peninsula following the drum must have given her the necessary skills to tend to a head wound. Neither she nor Mrs Burgoyne seemed unduly worried, but Bella was so very pale and deeply unconscious when I found her.'

'I can hear someone coming.' Emily rushed to the door and Aunt Jemima walked in and immediately smiled and nodded in his direction. 'She lost a deal of blood, but nothing that can't be remedied with a pint of warm, watered wine. Don't look so perturbed, my boy. Apart from the four stitches in her head, she will be fully recovered by tomorrow.'

His sister embraced her, and he surged to his feet, tempted to do the same. 'I cannot thank you enough for your help. There's no doctor available and . . . ' He couldn't continue; he was unmanned at the thought of what might have happened.

'Nonsense, my boy. Your timely intervention with your stock and kerchief was enough to prevent further loss of blood. She would have done perfectly well until the physician had arrived.'

Her brisk response was enough to steady him. 'Can I go up and see her?'

'She's awake now and asking for you, which is why I came down.'

He was out of the room and pounding up the stairs before she'd finished her sentence. Bella's bedchamber door stood open and he walked in.

# 12

Bella needed to reassure Simon that she'd been doing nothing he could be cross about when she'd had her accident. Her mama was sitting discreetly in the corner of the bedchamber when he burst in.

'I can't tell you how relieved I am to see you awake. Does your head hurt very much?'

'No, hardly at all. I was feeling faint and my foot slipped and that's how I came to knock myself out. I'm sorry to have delayed our departure and caused so much upset by my mishap.'

He ignored her parent, grabbed the nearest chair and pulled it close to the bed. 'You have nothing to apologise for. We shall stay here for another night and leave tomorrow morning.'

'No, there's no need for you to delay on my behalf. I'd much prefer it if you and your family continue to your home and not wait for me. Remaining might cause serious inconvenience to this place; I doubt they'll have enough rooms tonight as we were only booked for last night.'

He looked genuinely surprised that she should be bothered about such things. 'I'm sure they'll be only too happy to accommodate us and whoever loses their reservation will soon find somewhere else in the neighbourhood.'

Her mama spoke quietly from her position by the window. 'My lord, none of us have our servants or our luggage. Why would you wish to have your aunt and sister put in this position when it's not necessary? I can assure you that as soon as my daughter is well enough, we'll join you at your home.'

He shrugged. 'I see that I'm outmanoeuvred on this matter, ma'am, and agree to leave you here. Bella, I'm not happy to depart without you but will do so as it's what you wish me to do.'

He raised her hands and kissed the knuckles, stood up, nodded to her mother and strode from the room. As soon as he was gone, her mother took the place he'd vacated.

'Why do you look so worried, my love? Do you think he was displeased with you for sending him away?'

'He doesn't like being told what to do — but then what gentleman does? No, there's something I must tell you as it has been preying on my mind. I think I was unwell because I haven't eaten or drunk anything for twenty-four hours. I was so worried about an incident on my journey here.'

She explained her concerns and her mother looked grave. 'You're right to be bothered by what happened. I think it would be best if we didn't go to Sawsbury but changed direction and went to our estate. If, as you suspect, you were recognised, it will be easier for both of you if you're apart. Your papa must go to Town and speak to Lady Danbury — she will know if the gossip has resurfaced.'

'And what then? I cannot ask him to

honour our engagement and ruin his own family's reputation by so doing. On the other hand, if he's obliged to repay Papa then his financial woes will return.' She flopped back on the pillow, overwhelmed by the possible repercussions of her impulsive behaviour. Mama patted her hand.

'There's no need to concern yourself about that at the moment, Bella, but I can assure you that young gentleman won't suffer because of your indiscretion.'

She must have drifted off to sleep, as when she opened her eyes a second time, she was alone. If she sat up too quickly, her head spun, so she did it slowly. After using the item behind the screen, she tottered back to bed, too unwell to think about what might be happening at this very moment to her hopes and dreams.

Although her mother and Mrs Featherstone had been certain she'd not suffered a concussion, she thought they might be wrong: her eyes would no longer focus, and she felt she was about to cast up her accounts. She would do better safely in bed.

She was woken by someone shaking her shoulder. She opened her eyes to see a strange gentleman staring down at her.

'Good, good, I was becoming concerned when you would not rouse. I am Doctor Fletcher. You have suffered a concussion and must remain where you are for several days. You will recover swiftly and I doubt you'll have need of my attention again. I bid you both good day.'

Bella wasn't quite sure exactly what attentions she'd received from him but something more pressing needed answering first.

'How long have I been asleep?'

Her mother answered from the other side of the bed. 'Too long, my love. Annie and the other servants are now back here with us, as is our luggage. Your papa has returned to London but will be rejoining us in a day or two.'

Bella took a moment to assimilate this information. 'Then Lord Sawsbury is aware that I'm more seriously injured than he thought.'

'No, he galloped on ahead and was able to send them back before they'd done more than half the journey. I thought it better not to communicate with him until we know how things stand in Town.'

'Did he take Rufus with him?'

'I've no idea where your horse is at this moment. I think it the least of our worries at present.'

'I'm feeling much recovered and think we should leave immediately for home. I'm sure Papa can be contacted before he sets out in the wrong direction.'

'Not today, my love, but we'll leave at first light tomorrow. If there's a storm about to break over your head then it would be better if you were in the safety of your own abode.'

\* \* \*

The following morning, they left early, and Bella immediately regretted her decision to leave so soon after her accident. Being bounced and rattled as the wheels of the carriage dipped into potholes and ruts was decidedly unpleasant when one had a horrible headache.

The journey seemed interminable but she wanted to complete it in the day and not have to stay overnight again. As they were not changing the team, the coachman was obliged to travel slowly and stop twice to allow the horses to rest.

As before, the luggage had gone on ahead, and should arrive in good time for the servants to have everything unpacked when she and her mother arrived. She was feeling so unwell when the carriage finally rocked to a standstill that she needed the assistance of two footmen to get her upstairs to her apartment.

Annie was waiting. 'I'll soon have you comfortable in bed, miss.'

Bella raised and lowered her arms as instructed and tumbled beneath the covers with a sigh of relief. She fell asleep immediately and woke refreshed the following morning to find everything had changed.

* * *

Simon was unsurprised when a message arrived from Mrs Burgoyne to say that Bella and her family were no longer coming to Sawsbury Hall but going directly to their own establishment. This confirmed the worrying information he'd received from her father.

He went in search of his sister and found her busy reading the letters that had accumulated in their absence. Why they hadn't been sent on he'd no idea.

'I'm going to London . . . '

'Good heavens, we've only just returned from Town — why do you feel the need to rush back so soon?'

'Business matters: both Danbury and Burgoyne wish me to join them there immediately.'

'I see. Then it would have been better perhaps to have remained where we were and not have traipsed over the country like this.'

'You will remain here with Aunt Jemima as planned. By the by, Bella isn't coming here now but has returned to her own home with her mother.'

Her expression changed. 'This is worrying news indeed, brother, I sincerely hope that whatever catastrophe has occurred this time you can overcome it. You and Bella are made for each other and it will be a disaster if you cannot be married as you planned.'

'I intend to marry her and it's not because of the money. By some extraordinary happenstance I find myself in love with her; if I cannot have her as my wife then I'll not marry at all.'

She looked at him as if he had recently escaped from a lunatic asylum. 'Not marry at all? Have you run mad? The estates are entailed, and you have no legitimate heir.'

'I have no illegitimate ones either.' He hoped to make her smile but failed miserably.

'This is no time for jesting, Simon. You must tell me at once why you think you've been summoned to Grosvenor Square.'

He explained what he thought had occurred. 'I can't see it makes any difference if she was seen without an escort. Once she is your countess these rumours will no longer matter. I can assure you that I'd rather have fewer suitors because of the gossip than lose Bella as my sister.'

'I hoped you'd say that. It could well mean remaining here for a year or so to let the dust settle.'

'I'm in no hurry to leave — in fact, I think we should cancel my ball and hold some sort of celebration here.'

'The banns will have to be read at Sawsbury Church and not in London, but I hardly see that as a disadvantage.'

Aunt Jemima had wandered in as they were speaking and overheard the conversation. 'Forgive me for interfering, my boy, but I think whatever's going on you should hold to your original plans. Advance, my boy, never retreat.'

'I'll bear that in mind, ma'am, but if you will excuse me, I must make ready for my journey. I've decided to travel post-chaise as the matter appears to be urgent.'

'You must send word by express as soon as you know anything, Simon. Godspeed.'

★   ★   ★

Having never travelled this way before, as it was exorbitantly expensive, Simon was astonished at the speed they journeyed. They were aptly named as 'yellow bounders'. He pitied the postillion obliged to ride astride the lead horse. As the teams were changed every hour or so, the animals did not become distressed. He could not say the same for the passenger.

When eventually he disembarked outside his town house, he was bruised and battered and made a vow that in future, however urgent the business, he would not use this mode of transport a second time. Covering a distance that normally took a day and a half in a few hours was disconcerting.

His valet had been abandoned as this visit to the metropolis would not be for more than one night. He had left a wardrobe full of spare garments in Town so hadn't brought bags with him. Belatedly it occurred to him that his next destination might well be the home of his beloved, Hawksford Manor, and not his own estate. Too late to repine. He could manage perfectly well without his valet if needs be.

Despite his unexpected arrival, a footman opened the door and bowed him in. His young butler appeared almost immediately.

'Will you be staying long, my lord, or is this a flying visit?'

'Tonight, but probably no longer than that. Are there any messages for me?'

A silver salver appeared as if by magic, upon which were half a dozen letters. He nodded his thanks but didn't pick up his correspondence. 'Have coffee and whatever's available in the kitchen sent to my study in a quarter of an hour, along with these.'

The necessary hot water appeared in his chamber almost immediately. He stripped off his soiled stock and shirt, washed and replaced them with a crisply ironed shirt and starched neck-cloth. He was aware there was someone moving about in the dressing room behind him but he took no notice until his topcoat appeared sponged and ready to wear.

He shrugged into it whilst the willing footman rubbed his boots free of grime. He tossed the young man a silver six-pence and strode through the house to the study, where his impromptu meal had been set out on a damask tablecloth with all the accoutrements associated with a grand dinner.

He looked at the pile of letters and at the food from which a delicious aroma wafted. He would eat first, just in case one of the missives contained such bad news he lost his appetite. The hour was late, in fact the last twenty miles of his journey had been completed in darkness, so he was both impressed and astonished that his staff were able to cater to his needs so well.

He poured himself a third cup of coffee and carried it to the desk. He flicked through the letters and thought that four of them were from ladies, if he was any judge of handwriting. He opened the first of the other two. It was from his lawyer:

*My lord,*

*I regret to inform you that there has been further unpleasant gossip about Miss Burgoyne. She was seen and recognised by a group of young gentlemen at an inn some distance from London with only her groom for company.*

*As you can imagine, this coming so close to the first rumour has added fuel to the fire. I anticipate that you will wish to cancel your betrothal as in the circumstances you cannot possibly continue without permanently damaging the good name of your family.*

*I suggest that you visit my office at the earliest opportunity.*

Simon tossed the letter aside in disgust. How dare this man give him instructions? He was damned if he was going to go cap in hand to his lawyer, where the wretched man would obviously wish to arrange further loans so that the money he'd received from Burgoyne could be returned.

He would marry Bella and face the consequences and no one would tell him otherwise. He flicked open the red blob of sealing wax. This letter was from Danbury:

*Sawsbury,*
*No doubt by the time you're reading this you will already know that Bella's unwise decision to ride alone is now the talk of the Town.*

*What you don't know is that the information about the loss of the ships was premature — some foundered but a goodly portion of the fleet is safe and on its way to Liverpool.*

*My fortunes are now restored and I'm in a position to return the loan I had from your future father-in-law. I'm certain that you will ignore the opprobrium of the ton and go ahead with your marriage.*

*Burgoyne has gone to Liverpool so has asked me to call on you. Would you send word to Hanover Square on your arrival, whatever time of the day or night it might be? I shall come to you at once.*

The contrast between the two letters could not have been more marked. Danbury was a gentleman he intended to become better acquainted with. Should he send a footman even though it was already well after ten o'clock or could it wait until the morning?

As expected, the other letters were

expressing the regrets of the writer that they were no longer able to attend Emily's ball. He was torn — should he cancel all further engagements, including their own event, or continue as if nothing unseemly had happened? He didn't care if he was given the cut direct, if backs were turned on him as he approached, but he wouldn't put Emily or Bella through that humiliation.

His lips curved. He was quite certain Aunt Jemima wouldn't be fazed for one minute by anything that happened here. After all, had she not been present at a variety of battles and seen things that would shock even the stoutest heart?

He rang the bell and sent the footman who answered his summons to Hanover Square. He paced the study, trying to get his thoughts in order, and wished that his future father-in-law had put his daughter's welfare ahead of his business interests and remained to speak to him first.

Half an hour later, Danbury arrived. 'I didn't expect to hear from you until tomorrow at the earliest but I'm glad you're here.'

They shook hands and Simon poured them both a generous glass of cognac before they took their seats in front of the fire.

'My lawyer thinks I'll break off the engagement, but however bad the situation I intend to marry Bella. Not for the money, I hasten to add, but because I love her and no one else will do.'

'Good man, that's no more than I expected of you. I think it would be best to vacate this house and remain on your estate until after your nuptials. Why not hold a house party at Sawsbury Hall? My daughters were most impressed by the officers who attended our little soirée the other night and are content to abandon our plans for the Season if they can spend time flirting with those military gentlemen.'

'Mrs Featherstone thinks otherwise, but I agree with you. We don't want to put the ladies through any embarrassment if we can avoid it. My house is vast, a draughty mausoleum of a place, but there is an abundance of guest rooms and servants' quarters.'

'So you could accommodate everyone with ease?'

'If I take the staff from here then I think I can safely invite fifty or more. There is one small problem, however: I need to convince Bella that she must go ahead with the marriage.'

# 13

The next three days passed in a blur as Bella was barely awake. On the fourth day, she was roused by raised voices outside the bedchamber door. With some trepidation, she moved her head and was relieved to find it no longer hurt when she did.

One of the people outside was Simon. She braced herself for his arrival; he wouldn't allow anyone to keep him out once he'd decided to come in. Mama was vociferous in her efforts to stop him but he was having none of it. The door swung open and he stepped in.

Her mouth gaped and her eyes widened. What was so urgent that he'd come to her, travel-stained and in disarray? She raised a hand, stopping him in his tracks.

'No, I'll not speak to you in here. I

shall get up whilst you remove the dirt from your journey. Return in half an hour.'

His mouth thinned. He was not used to being given orders so abruptly. Then he nodded and departed as speedily as he'd arrived.

'My dear girl, I do apologise for that. I tried to tell him you were asleep, recovering from your concussion, but he wouldn't listen.'

'I'm well now, Mama, and I'm going to get up. I cannot dawdle as I'm certain he'll be here not a minute later than the time I gave him.'

Annie had sent the chambermaid running to fetch hot water and soon, with the assistance of her maid, Bella was feeling more the thing.

'My hair must remain loose as putting it up pulls horribly on the sutures.'

'I'll gather it loosely at your nape, miss, and tie it with a ribbon that matches your gown.'

As she was being dressed she'd had

time to review what had happened. Simon might be her future husband but he was a guest here and he'd showed appalling manners by intruding as he had.

The door crashed open just as she was stepping into her sitting room, adding to her annoyance. 'There's no need to bang doors like that, my lord. I can say with absolute certainty that everyone here is well aware of your displeasure without the necessity for you to behave like a schoolboy.'

This was hardly conciliatory, but at Hawksford she would be treated with respect.

He seemed to grow several inches to become a veritable giant, and a very angry one at that. She refused to be cowed, straightened her shoulders and glared right back at him.

'Miss Burgoyne, I have travelled here to assure you that despite everything that's being said to your detriment in Town, I intend to honour our arrangement.'

'Then you will be delighted to know that I am releasing you from your obligations. My father has agreed he will not require you to repay the money he has given you, as it is I that am breaking the engagement. I thank you for coming and hope that you eventually find someone less objectionable to marry.'

The words had come from nowhere, but, having spoken them, a weight lifted from her shoulders. Until that moment she'd not realised how she felt about marrying a gentleman she scarcely knew and wasn't sure she even liked.

If she'd expected him to protest, to try and persuade her to change her mind, she would have been bitterly disappointed. He bowed, as if to a lady that he didn't know.

'Breaking the arrangement is your prerogative, but until I have spoken to your father we must remain betrothed.'

There could be only one reason for his reluctance to sever the connection. 'Very well, but as far as I'm concerned, it's over. As you don't trust I'm speaking the truth about the money, I can understand your desire to have it confirmed.'

She nodded and stood rigid until he left the room. Where was Papa? Surely, he should be with them by now?

After a few minutes, she went in search of her mother and eventually discovered her in her own sitting room, busily writing a letter.

'Mama, where is Papa? Lord Sawsbury insists he must speak to him before he accepts our engagement is broken.'

'Papa is in Liverpool attending to some business. Whilst you were unwell we heard that only a portion of the fleet was lost and the remaining ships are on their way to England. He's gone to try and confirm that the information is correct.'

'Does that mean he's going to sail in search of them? He might be gone for months.'

'No, child, he hopes to speak to other

captains who might have seen or heard something on the subject and be able to confirm that everything was not lost.'

'I suppose his lordship will remain here in the meantime?'

'I am at this very moment writing to your father informing him of your decision. I'm certain he will write to you and to Lord Sawsbury as soon as he receives this. It will go by express and he should have it by the morning.'

The thought of sharing her home with him for the next few days filled her with foreboding. He was a very persuasive gentleman and might well attempt to change her mind.

'Mama, how bad is the gossip? Would marrying me taint the Sawsbury name?'

'It certainly wouldn't enhance it. That young man wishes to marry you regardless and despite your reservations, I don't think it's because of the funds.'

'Even if that were true, I no longer wish to be married — not to him or anyone. I know it will be a disappointment to you and Papa, but I think it best in the circumstances that I don't marry into the aristocracy after all.'

'Do you believe that your name is irredeemably blackened? That you'll never be accepted in the best drawing rooms?'

'No, I don't give a fig for that. I understand myself a little better now. Wealthy families who have made their money through hard work don't ostracise people in the same way as the *ton*. Sawsbury was at pains to explain that however bad my reputation might be at the moment, just by being married to him my sins would be expunged. When I marry it will be to somebody like us who doesn't live by such narrow-minded rules.' Mama didn't respond but merely smiled.

'I'm going for a walk around the garden. Why don't you come with me, my dear? The fresh air will do you good after being in bed for several days.'

The weather was surprisingly clement for the beginning of April. The roses were in bud, the trees were bursting with fresh, green leaves and birdsong filled the air. Bella loved the grounds of Hawksford, even though the house was far too large for such a small family.

*   *   *

Simon was staring from his sitting room window and saw Bella and her mother appear below. He didn't give a damn about speaking to her father; it was merely an excuse to remain under her roof and give him the opportunity to persuade her to change her mind.

He watched them for a few minutes and then decided to go out and join them. He wasn't sure how many days he had before he would be obliged to leave. Burgoyne could arrive at any moment and his excuse to linger would be gone.

He'd arrived in his carriage, his baggage on the back and his valet inside with him. His horses would need two days to recover and he intended to use every minute to his advantage.

He strolled out onto the terrace as the two ladies were returning up the handsome marble staircase that led from the gardens below.

'Mrs Burgoyne, Bella, may I walk with you a while?'

She was about to refuse but her mother smiled. 'I'm about to go inside; you take my place, my lord.'

Before Bella could protest, he stepped in and threaded her arm through his. 'It will do us both good to stretch our legs. The park is well laid out, did your father employ Capability Brown?'

'No, it was like this when we arrived.' She pointed into the distance where the crumbling turrets of a folly could be seen on the far side of the ornamental lake. 'That's my favourite place — I intend to walk there.'

'Then I'll accompany you. It must be more than a mile and you might need my assistance if you feel unwell at some point.'

She shrugged as if she cared not if he came or remained behind. 'I'm fully recovered, thank you, sir, but you may come if you insist.'

This was hardly an auspicious start to his campaign but he would have her to himself for at least an hour. They took the direct route across the huge expanse of grass. The hem of her gown was already mired but she seemed oblivious to this.

'I see you frowning at my gown, my lord. It matters not to me if it becomes dirty from my walk. There are more important things in life than worrying about a bit of honest mud.'

Her tone was clipped. Things had definitely changed between them and he was at a loss to know why she was behaving as if she cordially disliked him.

'You have sufficient servants to take care of such matters, no doubt. Emily has similar views as you and when at home in the country rakes about the place like a hoyden.' This comment made her look at him with more interest.

'And how do you feel about that? Do you take her to task for not conforming to the expected behaviour of a lady?'

'I don't give a damn what she does at Sawsbury. As long as she behaves in public I'm content.'

'Why is it, sir, that you may use appalling language in my presence and yet frown at my dirty skirts? I'm certain you would not dream of behaving so with someone from your own class.'

The worry that had been weighing him down lifted as he finally understood what bee had got into her bonnet. He halted, forcing her to do the same. The fact that they were in full view of the house and any outside men who might be in the grounds mattered not.

'Sweetheart, don't you see? I can be myself with you in a way I couldn't possibly be with a silly debutante from an aristocratic family. I apologise if my occasional lapse of language offends you, but . . . '

She no longer looked at him coldly but there was sadness in her eyes.

'Simon, I cannot marry you. Not just because my name is blackened, or that by marrying me you might well ruin Emily's chances of a suitable marriage, but because I don't want to marry anyone at the moment.

'In fact, I must tell you that when I do decide to wed it will definitely not be to a gentleman from the *ton* but from my own strata of society. I don't want my children to be forced to behave in a certain way in order to be accepted. I don't want my beloved parents to be looked down on and only tolerated by those they meet.'

'And if I give you my word that none of those things would happen, won't you reconsider?'

She shook her head, but there were tears glistening in her eyes. 'I like you very much, and it's breaking my heart to send you away, but it's the best thing for both of us. And certainly it will be far better for Emily not to be associated with me.'

His momentary elation was crushed

beneath her slippers. He could hardly reveal that he'd fallen in love with her, even if that meant she might change her mind. He had no intention of doing anything to cause her a moment's further distress.

'If you will permit me, I should still like to wait and speak to your father. I give you my word as a gentleman that I'll not importune you with my company.' He bowed formally and walked away, leaving his happiness behind.

His world had been stood on its head in the past two weeks and he needed time to adjust. He wished fervently that he'd never come to London — that he had not met Bella at all. He must accept that his engagement was now severed and that he was free to find himself another bride.

The thought of marrying anyone else filled him with horror. He was the last in his line so had no option but to marry at some point and provide an heir. This would not take place for some years but in the interim he must find a way of repaying Burgoyne for his generosity.

Thank God he was free of debt, because once word had spread around Town that he was no longer marrying an heiress, his credit would have been gone and the family ruined.

★ ★ ★

Bella watched him go and even knowing that she had done the right thing didn't make it any easier. He was as wretched as she about the whole business, but the only one to blame was herself. Whatever she'd said to the contrary to her mother, she would marry one particular aristocrat in a heartbeat if things were different.

The thought of marrying anyone else, whether from her own class or not, was something she couldn't contemplate at the moment — if ever. In that moment, she understood why she was so devastated to send him away. She was in love with him, despite his many faults, and no one else would do.

Angrily she brushed away her tears, picked up her skirts, and ran pell-mell towards the folly, where she knew she could be alone to come to terms with what she'd lost. She ran the whole distance, determined to prove to herself that at least she could do something properly.

Perspiration was trickling down her face, her lovely gown was quite ruined, and she could scarcely breathe her heart was pounding so fast, but for those mad minutes she'd been free of pain as all she'd been able to do was concentrate on reaching her goal.

The folly was equipped for visitors; it had comfortable seating inside and fresh water for both horses and humans. She tipped some into the basin and plunged her face into it. When she lifted it, she was cooler, but her hair had come loose, and this too was soaking wet.

She flicked out the remaining pins and ran her fingers through it, hoping to remove the worst of the tangles. There was a mirror somewhere if she recalled correctly, but she'd no need to look in it to see she was a disgrace.

She could not possibly return in daylight. Although she considered herself an independent and courageous person, even she could not face being seen returning through the grounds as she was. There was no option but to remain in the folly until dark and pray that no one sent out a search party for her, as that would be even more humiliating than being seen in her disarray.

The water had been standing in the pitcher for far too long to be safe to drink so she would have to remain thirsty and hungry, as well as dirty and wet, for the next few hours. Some small consolation was the fact that both her gown and her hair would have dried by the time she ventured forth. To facilitate this process, she made the bold decision to step out of her dress so she could drape it over the back of one of the chairs. Her hair would also dry more quickly if left loose.

There were rugs in the chest under the window and she removed them. With these wrapped around her, she could curl up on the large bed in the centre of the space and sleep the time away. She wondered why there was a bed in such a place. She glanced upwards and for the first time noticed there was a mirror on the ceiling. How extraordinary!

She looked like a dishevelled dryad with her red hair spread out around her and her arms and legs bare. Her mouth curved at the thought of what the tabbies would say if they saw her now. She was little better than a light-skirt in their opinion and this would just confirm their view.

It was comfortable snuggled beneath the covers and, notwithstanding the appalling circumstances she found herself in, she was able to drift off to sleep quite easily. When she woke, she was disorientated, and couldn't work out where she was for a moment.

Good grief! It was quite dark and she'd forgotten to put the tinderbox and candles by the bed so she could see what she was doing. She could hardly stumble about in pitch darkness in these unfamiliar surroundings, so she might as well remain here until dawn.

Hopefully her mama would think her in bed and no one would come in search of her before she was able to return safely to her own apartment. She was very hungry, but that was no more than she deserved. A bigger worry was her thirst, for having exerted so much energy running yesterday she was sorely in need of a drink.

With a sigh, she pulled the covers over her head for a second time, in the hope that she could drift off to sleep. If she was fortunate, her dry throat and empty stomach would not keep her awake. Maybe it would be light enough to escape when she opened her eyes again.

# 14

Hawksford Manor was almost as large as Sawsbury Hall, which meant one was able to remain invisible if one wanted to. Simon appeared at five o'clock, dressed in his evening rig for dinner, only to be told that no formal meal was to be served that night as both Bella and her mother were taking trays in their apartments.

'Serve me in the library. I'll have a bottle of claret if there is any.'

The butler nodded. 'Yes, my lord, the master keeps an excellent cellar. Do you have any preference for your dinner?'

'No, send whatever is available. Coffee and cognac afterwards, but no desserts.'

After returning from the stables, he'd spent the remainder of the afternoon in the library and had been mightily impressed by row upon row of leather-bound volumes. Many of them, on inspection, still had uncut pages so had never been read. No doubt they'd come with the purchase of the property.

He consumed the wine and food and then made serious inroads into the decanter of excellent brandy. Drowning his sorrows with alcohol was hardly a sensible move and if he retired in his cups he would wake with a headache. There were windows at the far end of the library, and he carried his candle there to see if he could open one and climb out into the grounds, without the necessity of finding a footman to unlock a door.

He pushed it up, the rattle of the sashes loud in the darkness. He hoped no one thought he was a burglar coming in, rather than a guest climbing out. He swung his legs over the sill and let go.

He'd expected to drop no more than a few feet, but to his horror he fell double that distance. There was no time to adjust and his right ankle gave way beneath him when he hit the ground. He bit back his yell of agony and was unable to move for several minutes until the pain subsided.

Devil take it! He feared he'd broken it as the pain was so intense. Even the slightest movement made his head spin. He inched his way backwards on his elbows until he reached the wall. Hopefully he could use this to brace himself and get into a sitting position.

What a damn fool thing to do — if he'd not been half-drunk he would have thought to check how far it was to the ground before he'd jumped out. The library was at the rear of the building, somewhere he'd not ventured on his earlier walk, so he'd not been aware that the ground dropped away so catastrophically on this side.

He smiled ruefully. At least he was sober now, which was the reason he'd wanted to come out into the fresh air in the first place. He doubted if he'd be able to rouse anyone even if he shouted.

Unless he could hoist himself to his feet and hop the entire length of the house, he was obliged to remain where he was until light.

His ankle hurt like the very devil and already damp was seeping through the double thickness of his coat-tails and evening trousers. He shivered and all desire to smile evaporated. This situation was far from amusing. He had two choices and neither of them appealed to him. He could remain where he was until light and risk catching a congestion of the lungs, or somehow make his way to the front door and possibly cause irreversible damage to the injured limb.

After sitting and weighing up his options, he decided he might as well try shouting a few times — he had nothing to lose if nobody came and everything to gain if they did. As expected, the house remained closed despite his best efforts, which left him with the two unpalatable choices.

Then, to his astonishment, he heard

Bella calling his name. Her voice was faint but just discernible as sound carried wonderfully at night. 'Simon, Simon, is that you shouting for help? Where are you? I've no lantern and there's no moon so I cannot see you.'

'I'm on the ground below the library window,' he yelled. 'I've broken my ankle and cannot move.'

The reply was clearer. 'I'm on the terrace now but am going to wake the house before I come to you. I won't be able to get you inside on my own.'

Now he knew rescue was imminent, he began to think how he could explain his predicament without seeming a complete nincompoop. He wasn't exactly sure how long he'd been sitting there but he knew he was damn cold and his rear end had gone quite numb.

He didn't know if it was a good thing or not that the pain in his ankle had diminished somewhat since he'd fallen. There was the sound of running steps approaching and the flicker of a swaying lantern. Bella appeared from around the corner and close behind her were a positive army of servants, carrying what looked like a trestle and a bundle of rugs.

'I won't ask how you come to be here, my lord. That can wait until later.' She held the lantern close to his face and then moved it down to his feet. This was the first time he'd seen the injury himself. He was shocked when he saw the peculiar angle of his right foot.

'As you can see, you've broken your ankle. I've brought the necessary splints and bandages to secure it whilst you're moved. The doctor has been sent for and by the time we've got you inside, he should be here.'

She sounded brisk, impersonal even, and her calmness made him love her more. Any other young lady would be collapsed in a heap of tears and recriminations, not dealing with matters so efficiently.

She knelt beside him and only then did he recognise his valet, Mason, was beside her. 'I'm going to cut off your boot, my lord, then straighten your foot.' His man handed him a strip of leather to bite on.

Simon braced himself. The agony just from having his boot removed was even worse than he'd anticipated. Then a merciful blackness enveloped him and he knew no more.

★   ★   ★

'Quickly, Mason, he's unconscious. I'll hold his leg whilst you do what you must.' He'd assured her it wasn't the first time he'd been asked to set a break and she trusted him not to make matters worse. They could hardly transport Simon safely until the break was splinted and that wouldn't be possible with his foot facing in the wrong direction.

She averted her gaze whilst the limb was straightened. Splints were tied on either side of Simon's leg and then he was ready to be transferred to the waiting trestle. Four willing footmen, in various states of disarray, carefully lifted the patient onto the board.

'There's a small apartment on the ground floor, once used by an ancient relative of the previous owner. I've had that prepared for Lord Sawsbury.'

The French doors that led into the drawing room were now wide open, which meant they didn't have to carry the unconscious man the length of the house and back again in order to access these rooms. The house was now ablaze with light. The housekeeper, immaculate as always, curtsied as they entered.

'Miss Burgoyne, everything is ready for his lordship. His trunk has been transferred and the bed freshly made up.'

'Is the fire lit? Are there bricks in the bed?'

'Yes, miss; both have been done.'

Bella wanted to remain, to assist in any way she could, but this was impossible. His man and two of the footmen must undress Simon, put on his warm nightshirt and place him in his temporary bed.

The housekeeper touched her arm. 'Miss Burgoyne, it will take some time to make his lordship comfortable. Perhaps you would like to change into something warmer yourself.'

For a moment, Bella didn't understand, but then stared down at her crumpled, dirty gown. 'I'll do so immediately.'

She took the secondary stairs, those used by guests staying in the chambers above, and raced to her own rooms. She was surprised but delighted to find Annie waiting for her. The girl's eyes were red.

'Heavens, whatever is wrong? I'm sure his lordship is in no danger.'

'Oh, miss, when I found your bed hadn't been slept in, I was beside myself.' The girl turned scarlet, hesitated, and then continued. 'I thought perhaps you were sleeping elsewhere tonight but I should have raised the alarm. I'm ever so sorry . . . '

'There's no need to apologise. I'm glad you didn't set up a search for me. I walked to the folly and then fell asleep.

When I woke I thought it too dark to come back. Then I heard his lordship calling out.'

'Thank the good Lord that you did so, miss, because — '

'That's quite enough. I wish to return downstairs immediately.'

Her maid deftly removed the ruined gown and dropped a fresh one over her head. Then Annie restored Bella's hair to its normal tidy appearance and she was ready to depart. The entire procedure had taken less than twenty minutes.

She returned by the same route and arrived at the apartment with the physician. Although they had resided here for three years, they had never had recourse to call on his services before. He was a young man and she hoped this made it more likely he was skilled in modern practices and wouldn't wish to bleed or purge the patient.

When she explained what had transpired, he nodded and said tersely. 'I hope your interference didn't make matters worse.' Hardly a polite response, but it gave her confidence he knew what he was about.

He strode into the bedchamber, leaving her pacing anxiously in the adjoining sitting room for what seemed like several hours, but was in fact only one.

The housekeeper appeared, carrying a welcome tray of coffee and sandwiches. 'I thought you might be in need of refreshment, miss.'

'I'd forgotten how hungry and thirsty I was — thank you so much. By the way, what is the name of the doctor you called?'

'Doctor Sampson, miss, he bought the practice a year ago and is well thought of in these parts.'

Despite the fact she was tormented by worry, she demolished the food and drank the entire pot of coffee. When eventually the bedchamber door opened and the doctor emerged, she was feeling much restored.

He forestalled her question by speaking first. 'Lord Sawsbury was lucky to have been found so quickly. Also, I'm glad to report that, rather than damaging the patient, the treatment he received from his valet will make his recovery much speedier.'

'I'm relieved to hear you say so, Doctor Sampson. How long will it be before his lordship can be moved somewhere more appropriate?'

'He must remain where he is for three weeks if his ankle is to set properly and not leave him lame. I'm confident he will not suffer any ill effects from his being outside and he'll make a full recovery in time.'

'Thank you. I take it that you'll be visiting every day.' This wasn't a question but a statement.

'I shall. I understand from his lordship that you intend to be married soon, but that will have to be postponed. However, I'm sanguine he'll be fully recovered by June so I should reset the day for then.'

She opened her mouth to deny they were betrothed but it was none of the doctor's business. 'I bid you good night, sir; thank you again for your prompt and efficient attendance.'

She remained standing in the centre of the room, unable to quite comprehend what had just been said. Good heavens! Simon must be conscious and had told the doctor they were still betrothed.

She rushed into his bedchamber to see for herself that he was not at death's door as she'd feared earlier. He was propped up in bed and looked remarkably cheerful for a man with such a serious injury. There was a cage of some sort, protecting his leg from the covers.

'Good, I was hoping you would come and see me. It seems I owe my life to you.'

There was a chair already waiting for her at the head of the bed and she took it. 'That's doing it too brown, sir, but I'm glad I was of some assistance.'

He reached out and took her hand; when she tried to remove it, his grip tightened. 'No, Bella, be still. Tell me what you were doing outside fully clothed in the middle of the night.'

There was no point in giving him a Banbury tale, she might as well be honest. 'I ran all the way to the folly and was then so exhausted I stretched out on the bed to sleep. When I awoke it was dark . . . '

'That doesn't explain why your hair was loose.' His tone was bland but there was something strange about his expression. For a moment she was puzzled by his attitude but then she understood.

She tried to remove her hand but he refused to relinquish it. He was openly laughing now and if he wasn't an invalid, she would throw something at him.

'There's only one reason anyone visits that folly; are you so naïve you did not realise the significance of there being a bed and a mirrored ceiling?'

She stopped struggling and stared at him. Then colour flooded from her toes to her crown and she squirmed in her chair. With lowered eyes, she replied. 'I did think it odd but not until you drew my attention to it did I realise why it was so arranged.' Then she recalled what Annie had said about the empty bed. 'My maid thought I was with you so didn't raise the alarm . . . '

'And I got so drunk I jumped out of the window and broke my ankle. Whatever your feelings on the matter, Bella, I cannot leave here for several weeks.'

He didn't sound at all worried by this prospect. This reminded her of what the doctor had said.

'And that's another thing, sir: how could you tell a complete stranger that we're betrothed when you know very well that I severed the connection?'

'Accept the inevitable, sweetheart. If your maid thought you had come to me then what little reputation you had left will be gone. Also, my name will be blackened beyond repair if I do not do the honourable thing. A gentleman does not seduce a young lady.'

'Fiddlesticks to that! We both know that nothing of the kind happened . . . '

'We shall have the banns called in your family chapel this Sunday and be married as soon as I can stand upright. I shall send word to Emily and Aunt Jemima to join us here and also for Lord Danbury and his family. Hopefully your father will have returned in time to walk you down the aisle.'

It was a *fait accompli*. She must accept the inevitable and marry this man, whether she wished to or not. By some twist of fate, their lives were now inextricably tangled together and neither of them had a choice in the matter.

'I see I have no alternative but to agree. At least we will get to know each other better before we're wed. This is all such a muddle and I wish that I'd not fallen into your arms two weeks ago.'

He was stroking her palm with his thumb and, although the sensation was strange, for some reason she was reluctant to remove her hand from his.

'Go to bed, my darling. We both need to sleep.'

As she was rising, he pulled her, and she toppled forward. She couldn't struggle for fear that she would further

279

injure his ankle. Her head was resting on his shoulder; he gently turned her face towards him and then pressed his lips to hers.

'My lord, I have the tisane here to help you sleep.' His valet spoke from behind her.

'Thank you, Mason. Miss Burgoyne and I have settled on a wedding date.'

Bella scrambled to her feet and was almost certain she heard his man mutter, 'The sooner the better, I'd say.'

She left the room, not sure if she was happy or not that she was going to marry this charismatic gentleman. The fact that she loved him would make things a little easier for her, but what about him? He desired her but he didn't reciprocate her feelings — would this be enough to make him content with this ill-matched union?

With his leg broken, he would be unable to interfere with her life. That meant she had a few weeks of independence left, and she intended to make the most of it.

# 15

Simon was determined to get married long before June, even if he had to hobble on crutches or be wheeled in a bath chair. He spent the next two days writing letters to set things in motion and was unsurprised that his darling girl was conspicuous by her absence.

His future mother-in-law visited on the third day. 'I apologise for my daughter, my lord, she is remiss in her duties by not coming. I'm delighted that the wedding is now confirmed, and I've started making arrangements for the ceremony to be held as soon as you're able to move.'

'The doctor is happy with the progress of the injury. There is no infection and already the pain is bearable. If I continue to improve as I am, he said I can get out of bed next week, as long as I sit on the *chaise longue* and don't go anywhere else.'

'Your man is intending to search the attics for a bath chair today. I'm hopeful he'll be successful as these rooms were used by an elderly gentleman and he quite possibly could have had one.'

'Have you heard when Mr Burgoyne is to return, ma'am?'

'The last missive I received said he remained in Liverpool and that the news was encouraging. When do you expect your family to arrive?'

'They will be here in a day or two — I'm sure my sister is eager to see for herself that my injury isn't life-threatening. Lord Danbury and his family will also be here by the following weekend. I'm determined to tie the knot as soon as possible.'

She smiled. 'Bella is galloping about the country on the horse you bought for her. She insists that you will not allow her to ride astride once you're married and she intends to enjoy herself for as long as she is able.'

'I'd like to speak to her. Do you think

you could persuade her to come? If you assure her that I have no objection to her riding any way she chooses as long as it's within your park, or mine, she might be prepared to visit.'

'My daughter is headstrong, wilful even, but if she didn't want to marry you, believe me, she would refuse to continue the arrangement despite the circumstances.'

★　★　★

He was obliged to wait until the following morning before he got the promised visit. She hesitated in the door, as if not sure of her reception.

'Come in, Bella. My life's been decidedly dull without your company.' He pointed to her forehead. 'I think the stitches have come out — did my doctor attend to that?'

'He did. I'm most impressed with him. I hear Mason has discovered a chair for you and is at this very moment having it repaired.'

'I cannot use it to leave this apartment for another two weeks but I can transfer to my sitting room soon. I'm surprised my sister and Aunt Jemima are not here already.'

'We received a note today that they will be arriving by the weekend. It seems your aunt had business in Town to attend to before they came.'

He realised at once what was afoot. 'Devil take it! She will be inviting the officers and their families to your house. I should have mentioned it to your mama but it slipped my mind. Do you have the staff to deal with fifty or more guests plus their servants?'

'This place is the size of a palace. I don't believe that I've visited more than half the rooms in the three years we've lived here. It's always cold, even in the summer. I know my parents will be delighted to get rid of it and live somewhere sensible. Are they still to come to your Dower House?'

'Of course; nothing has changed apart from the venue for our wedding.

I'm glad we had the opportunity to waltz together as it might well be some time before we can stand up again.'

He hadn't asked her to draw nearer and take the seat beside his bed but during the conversation she'd drifted closer. She picked up the chair and moved it out of his reach before sitting.

'I'm sorry for the trouble I've caused by my behaviour . . . '

'There's no need to apologise, sweetheart, it's forgiven and forgotten. I can hardly hold you to account after breaking my ankle in such a ridiculous fashion.'

Her remarkable eyes sparkled and her smile was radiant. 'I would say it serves you right for getting drunk, if you hadn't injured yourself so grievously.' She hesitated, looked from side to side before speaking again. 'I want you to know that whatever the outcome of your injury I'll consider myself honoured to be your wife.'

Until the words, he'd not considered the possibility that he might be permanently damaged, that the young doctor might be wrong in his assessment of the situation.

He held out his hand but she hesitated and remained where she was. She was like an unbroken filly, not quite ready to accept the bit, and would need gentle handling until she was.

'I can't tell you how bored I am stuck here with nothing to do. Do you play chess?'

'I do, but I warn you I am an expert and rarely beaten.'

'Excellent. All we need now is the board, the pieces and the table upon which to put it.'

She jumped up. 'You stay where you are, sir, I'll fetch what we need.' He heard her laughing as she rushed off to acquire the necessary items.

He rang the small brass bell beside his bed. When Mason appeared, he sent him in search of a suitable table and to fetch coffee and pastries from the kitchen.

'When will my transport be ready?'

'Another day or two, my lord, no sooner.'

Simon was certain the bath chair would remain unavailable until Doctor Sampson agreed he could use it. Hopefully that would be next week. Being inactive did not suit him and he thought by the time he was allowed to escape this temporary prison he might well become irascible. His lips curved. Well — more irascible than usual.

★   ★   ★

Bella thought that playing chess with Simon was the perfect solution to the problem of visiting him and possibly being enticed into his embrace. With him on the far side of the card table, she was out of his grasp and all they could do was converse.

They played several games and the score was even when she finally left his room. 'You need to rest; all the laughing and talking cannot be good for your recovery.'

287

His smile made her heart jump. 'On the contrary, my love. I shall recover far quicker in your company than I could mouldering here on my own. Will you come to visit again today?'

'No, I've spent several hours here already. There are things Mama needs me to assist her with in order to prepare for our influx of visitors. I shall come after my ride tomorrow.'

When she looked back, he was already asleep. She saw his valet busy in the adjoining dressing room and beckoned him out. 'I've no wish to tire the patient, Mason. You must tell me if I'm overstaying my welcome.'

'The doctor said as long as he remains in bed he can do whatever he wants. The more you stay with him the better; I've never seen him in better spirits than when you're at his side, miss.'

'Thank you for taking such good care of him for me.'

There was no necessity to thank a servant for doing their job, but this man was close to Simon and was serving him through affection as much as duty.

Her mother greeted her with enthusiasm when she eventually located her in the small drawing room at the rear of the building, adjacent to the library. 'I was just about to send for you, my dear. I've heard from your papa and he will soon be on his way from Town. He should be with us in a day or so.'

'Was his trip successful, do you know?'

'Indeed it was. Two thirds of the fleet should dock in Liverpool next month. He's delighted that the wedding is to go ahead and believes he has already a buyer for this estate.'

'So soon? Does that mean you will move to Sawsbury when I leave with Simon?'

'That decision will be made by your father. Improvements and redecorations must be done to the Dower House before we can live there.'

'My new home, I'm assured, is even bigger than this and there will be ample room for you both until the refurbishment is completed. We'd intended to visit the Lake District and Scotland for our wedding trip but obviously that will no longer be possible. I don't even know if Simon will be fit to travel after our wedding.'

'On the subject of your nuptials, my love, I have everything in hand. All I require of you is that you check that the number of guest rooms prepared matches the number of people we are expecting.'

'As I've no idea how many are coming apart from Simon and Lord Danbury's family, I will find that difficult. Do you have a list?'

'His lordship was only able to give me a very rough estimate as he had no clear idea of the exact number of single gentlemen who will be amongst those coming. Imagine having a house full for the first time, and the majority of those will be military families.'

'Have you any events planned for the house party, apart from my wedding, of course?'

'The gentlemen can play billiards and the ladies can gossip during the day. In the evenings we will dine formally and then there can be cards and dancing.'

'I'm certain the officers will want more interesting things to do than play billiards. Would you have any objection if I organised some outdoor activities?'

Her mother was not so easily gulled. 'Exactly what do you have in mind, Annabel?'

'Some horse races around the park for one, and there are several punts in the boathouse so those could be put out ready for use. What about a treasure hunt of some sort? Simon and I can come up with the clues and be the adjudicators.'

'Unless some of the gentlemen arrive on horseback, there won't be sufficient mounts for them. However, I've no objection to any of your suggestions. What do you think would be suitable for the ladies of the party?'

'They can take part in the treasure hunt and the punting — I intend to join in the horse racing and I'm sure that Lady Emily will also wish to participate.'

'If you wish to dance every night let us hope there is someone in the party who can play the piano.'

'I can do so. As Simon cannot dance, then I shall not either.'

'I'm quite content to play as well, so that's the evening entertainment dealt with.'

* * *

The next two days passed in similar fashion, and the more time she spent with her future husband, the happier she was with the arrangement. The doctor pronounced his patient well enough to be transferred to the sitting room and, by a strange coincidence, the bath chair appeared the very same day in perfect working order.

Bella curtailed her morning ride in order to visit Simon the moment he was established in his new position. She had hoped to catch him in his indoor vehicle but he was already stretched out, fully clothed, on the daybed. The only difference to his normal appearance was the lack of a boot on his injured leg. They were interrupted by Mason with a message that the Sawsbury carriage was, at that very moment, trundling up the drive.

'Will you be able to join us for dinner tonight?'

'I haven't decided, but I'll ask the doctor when he calls later today. I am eager to see my sister; will you be kind enough to bring her to me as soon as she arrives?'

'I'll do that, but I expect she'll wish to change from her travelling gown before she comes here.'

She rushed out, as impatient as he was, to meet the visitors. Simon might not be aware of this, but apart from himself there had been no guests at all at Hawksford. Mama was already in the hall waiting to greet their new friends.

'It's so long since I've entertained,

I'm quite nervous. I cannot imagine what is keeping your papa from us for so long. His last letter assured me he was about to set off from London.'

'He'll be here soon, don't fret, Mama. I'm glad Simon's family didn't come whilst he was still bedridden — he looks more like himself now he's correctly dressed. I'm hoping he'll join us for dinner.'

The front door was open and Bella watched the carriage rock to a halt. Two footmen were there to let down the steps and escort the visitors inside. Only then did she wonder about Emily and Aunt Jemima's abigails and baggage — surely that should have arrived ahead of them?

The older lady descended closely followed by Emily, then the two dressers. They had obviously travelled together in the carriage. The more she knew about his family, the better she liked them; they apparently didn't have a rigid approach to etiquette and society rules.

'Welcome, Mrs Featherstone, Lady Emily, I hope you had a pleasant journey,' Mama said politely and she curtsied.

Emily rushed forward and took her hands. 'Please don't stand on ceremony, ma'am, for soon I'll be part of your family.'

'Emily, what kept you so long from us? I hope nothing untoward has occurred, for there's been enough disaster and excitement already.'

She embraced her friend and then curtsied to Aunt Jemima. 'The housekeeper will show you to your rooms, then Simon is eager to see you, Emily.'

'Take me to him immediately, he'll not mind if I'm travel-worn.'

Arm in arm they hurried down the endless, chilly passageways to the rear of the building. Emily drew her to a halt as they approached the door.

'How is he, really?'

'He's absolutely fine apart from his broken ankle.'

'I'm so relieved to hear you say so. I

have so much to tell you. Come in with me, so I don't have to repeat myself.'

★ ★ ★

Simon braced himself for the arrival of his sister. It was uncanny how alike she and his future wife were — was this why he'd fallen in love with Bella? Whatever the reasons, his feelings were growing stronger by the day and he intended to reveal them to her after their wedding.

Emily erupted into the room and was about to fling herself into his arms but remembered at the last minute that he had a broken ankle. 'You fraud! Here I am beside myself with worry at your condition and I find you looking perfectly well.'

He chuckled. 'Perfectly well apart from a badly broken ankle. Sit down and tell me you why you've taken so long to arrive.'

Bella glanced in his direction and her smile gave him hope that possibly she'd developed feelings for him too. She took a seat some distance from him, thus allowing his sister to take the chair meant for her.

'Aunt Jemima and I had to cancel all our engagements and send notes to those who had accepted the invitation to my ball. Then we arranged for your staff to close the house and to transfer themselves and your belongings to Sawsbury.

'Then we sent out new invitations to come here to those that had supported us at the Danbury's soirée. You must understand that we were obliged to wait until we had replies, so Mrs Burgoyne can know how many to expect next week.'

'Did any of them refuse because of the new gossip attached to my name?'

'Everyone who was invited has accepted. There will be seven single officers, some more eligible than others, plus six more with their families. Aunt Jemima is at this very moment discussing the list of names with your mama.'

'The house is prepared for fifty guests but I dare say we could accommodate more if necessary.'

'Bella, do you have the necessary staff? I can have those working in London come here instead of Sawsbury if that would help?'

'Thank you for your kind thought, but Papa took on everyone in the neighbourhood without employment, whether we needed them or not. We are shockingly overstaffed and this will be the first time in three years some of them will actually earn their wages.'

Bella explained to both of them what was being planned to entertain the influx of people. Simon wasn't happy about the prospect of her racing against men but knew better than to forbid it. He regretted this decision when his sister decided she too would take part in this event if she could find a suitable horse.

'Are you inviting any of your neighbours?'

She shook her head. 'I explained to you, Simon, that the toplofty folks around here want nothing to do with us. You will probably be astonished to hear that you are the first person, apart from the vicar and squire, to visit us.'

'That will be different once we're married. I'm sure your parents will also find friends when they are settled with us.'

Bella stood up and shook out the skirts of her pretty leaf green muslin. 'Forgive me, both of you, but I must go to my mama and see if there's anything that still needs doing. When did you say the first of the guests are arriving, Emily?'

'Not until next Friday, which gives us ample time to write the clues for the treasure hunt and arrange everything else. You are going to hold a celebration ball on your wedding day, I hope?'

'I've no idea what's been arranged, Emily, but I would certainly like to mark the occasion. What do you think, sweetheart?'

'We've never used the ballroom — in fact we've only used but two of the main reception rooms. I can't tell you how much I'm looking forward to seeing them opened up.'

She dashed off in a flurry of skirts, leaving him alone with his sister. As soon as the door closed, her happy smile faded.

'I couldn't tell you the true state of affairs when Bella was here. I've no wish to overset her.'

He pushed himself more upright on the daybed. 'Go on, tell me the worst. But before you do, you need to know that the marriage will go ahead regardless.'

'Whatever you think at this moment, I fear you might wish you could change your mind. I know you and Bella will be married but it's better to know than to be left in ignorance.'

'For God's sake, stop prevaricating and tell me what's being said.'

'Bella is now accused of meeting a lover at that hostelry. They say the hurried wedding is because she's in an interesting condition and the child is not yours. They say you are so desperate for money you're prepared to take on another man's bastard . . . '

He wasn't sure which shocked him more, the information or the fact that his sister was prepared to discuss it so openly.

'It's bad, but as there will be no baby in eight months' time that particular salacious piece of gossip will be proved inaccurate. I don't give a damn about any of it, but more to the point, do you? It's going to affect you more than it will us — it could well ruin your chances of making a successful marriage.'

'I don't give a fig about that. Aunt Jemima said that in twelve months it will have been forgotten and someone else will be the topic of conversation in the drawing rooms of the *ton*.'

'Then we shall ignore it and concentrate on the celebrations ahead. It's a damned nuisance about my ankle, it makes everything so much more complicated.'

'Tell me, brother, exactly how did this accident take place?'

# 16

Bella was about to retreat to her apartment to begin her preparations for dinner when she received a message that Simon wished to see her urgently. Her stomach lurched. Had the news from London been so appalling he wished to cancel their nuptials after all?

Then she recovered her equilibrium. Mama and Mrs Featherstone would not be so enthusiastic about the house party if the wedding was to be cancelled. Papa had arrived an hour ago and had been closeted with her mother ever since. She had not had a moment to speak to him herself as she'd been busy writing the clues for the treasure hunt with Emily.

Still in her green muslin — she refused to change in the middle of the day unless it was into a riding habit — she made her way to the ground floor chambers. The place was positively crawling with unfamiliar faces getting everything ready for next week.

Every single guest room, as well as those normally reserved for family, would be in use. All the rooms in the attics and in the servants' quarters below stairs would also be filled to capacity. There was a constant trundle of diligences arriving from the nearby town, as well as the village and local farms, bringing in the necessary supplies to feed so many extra mouths.

Fortunately, there was ample room in the stables for those horses that must be kept inside and those that were hardier could be turned out into the nearby home paddock.

She hesitated outside Simon's sitting room, unwilling to go in in case she heard the worst possible news, though she knew this was extremely unlikely. Was now the time to tell him that she loved him, or would this just exacerbate matters?

Somehow, he'd sensed her presence and called out cheerfully, 'Stop dithering about out there, my love, and come in. We don't have long before you must get changed for dinner.'

'Why the urgent message? What was it you needed to say to me that couldn't wait until later?'

'I wanted to be sure that you're not too concerned about the further damage to your reputation and to assure you I don't give a fig for it.'

'Aunt Jemima has assured me that it will be stale news in a week or two. Once we're married and I'm your countess I'll be of higher status than most of those that are gossiping now. The only thing that concerns me is the fact that you'll be unable to go to your clubs.'

He raised an eyebrow. 'Why should I not visit them?'

'It would be far too risky; a gentleman in his cups is bound to insult me and then you'll feel obliged to call him out and would be arrested or possibly hung for murder.'

His delighted laughter filled the room. 'In which case, my love, I'll take your advice and remain with you at Sawsbury.'

He gestured to his splints. 'By the time I'm able to go to Town I doubt that anyone will even remember.'

'I can't wait to see you being pushed about in that contraption. Have you asked Mason to cut the leg of your evening trousers?'

'Certainly not. I'm not changing for dinner. As it's only family at the table I doubt anyone will object. No, don't frown. I can assure you I'll be correctly attired by the time our guests arrive. I gather your father is now home — I'd hoped he would come to see me but as yet he hasn't.'

Papa spoke from behind her. 'I'm here now, my boy, but cannot remain more than a few minutes.'

She was tempted to stay in order to hear what had kept him away so long, but both gentlemen looked at her pointedly. She laughed and dashed off, leaving them to discuss their business in private. Mama would tell her what she knew and there was just time to visit her before returning to her own apartment.

On knocking, she was bid to enter. 'Quickly, child, come in so I can tell you why your father was delayed.'

'He's speaking to Simon at this very moment and I was sent away.'

'Apart from the unpleasant rumours circulating in London about you and Lord Sawsbury, all of it is good news. Papa was signing the papers which will transfer this place to the new owners in June. He also visited Sawsbury Hall and the Dower House and had set in motion the necessary refurbishments for our new abode. He tells me it's a delightful property, has half a dozen bedchambers, three reception rooms and excellent stabling. Although it's part of the park, it also has its own private garden so I can continue to grow my roses.'

She flung her arms around her mother. 'I find my feelings towards him have changed — I won't embarrass him by revealing that I love him, but because I do it's going to make it much easier for me.'

'I knew the moment I set eyes on him

that he was perfect for you. Run along, Bella, and get changed; it would not do for either of us to be tardy tonight.'

The gown she'd selected had a pale green silk underskirt and the overdress was of golden sparkles. Her slippers were golden too and there were matching green and gold ribbons threaded through her elaborate hair arrangement.

She scarcely recognised herself in the long glass. 'I look so grown-up, Annie. Isn't it amazing what a fine gown can do to one's appearance?'

Her maid adjusted the gold wrap around her shoulders, smoothed out the skirts of the gown and carefully hooked the small loop of silk, that would hold up the demi-train, over her waiting wrist.

Emily and Mrs Featherstone had rooms on this side of the house, and she hesitated in the passageway, not sure if they'd gone down already. After a few moments she decided it would be better if she proceeded on her own.

She paused at the head of the grand staircase that swept in a magnificent curve of intricately carved oak from the gallery to the hall. She caught her breath and her pulse skittered. He was waiting for her in his chair. He'd lied: somehow his valet had adapted his evening clothes so he could wear them, and he looked quite magnificent despite the fact that he was seated.

His eyes blazed and she couldn't look away. She was obliged to grasp the banister to steady herself before she descended. There was no sign of his man, or indeed of anyone else, although she could hear voices coming from the drawing room.

'Darling girl, you've never looked more beautiful. Forgive me my small deception, I wanted to surprise you.' He held out his hand and her feet moved of their own volition until she was standing beside him.

She was so flustered she said the first thing that came into her head. 'Are you expecting me to push you in this thing? I doubt that I can do it successfully, dressed as I am.'

He reached out and took her hand. 'Mason is lurking somewhere.' He snapped the fingers on his free hand and, sure enough, his valet arrived.

★ ★ ★

As far as Simon was concerned, Bella's pink cheeks and rapid pulse were a good sign. They demonstrated that she found him desirable even if she hadn't quite fallen in love with him.

'Shall we join the others in the drawing room? I've no idea what sort of dinner will be served as we've never entertained before.'

'Everything I've eaten so far has been delicious so I don't think you've anything to worry about. I expect you already know that this house is sold.'

'Mama told me. I wish now we'd gone to your house so I had some idea what my future home looks like.'

'It's of similar vintage to this place, too large and too cold. With your permission I'll raze it to the ground and build us something smaller with all the modern conveniences.'

'Are you asking because the expense will be met by my inheritance? There's no need to have my approval. As your wife all I have belongs to you anyway.'

He was still holding her hand and she didn't seem eager to remove it. 'Good God!' He couldn't keep back his exclamation of astonishment when he saw the extraordinary ensemble Aunt Jemima had appeared in.

'Hush, I think she looks perfectly splendid. I'm sure she'll wear something more conventional when we have guests here.'

'I sincerely hope so. The plethora of bead fringing on all her garments is not only noisy but reminds me of a Romany.'

'There you are, my boy, I can see that you're not enamoured by my garments. Are you worried that I'll wear them to your nuptials?'

'I admit that I was somewhat startled by the . . . by the bright colours, but now I'm accustomed to them I find them quite attractive.'

A choking sound beside him almost set him off too. Fortunately, his sister stepped into the situation and began discussing the forthcoming treasure hunt.

Mason wheeled him into the dining room and then hovered to see if he'd be needed. Simon was able to lift himself from the bath chair with comparative ease. He was certain he heard a collective sigh of relief as he settled himself at the table.

The food was excellent but he drank little and he was glad that Bella only took one glass of wine all evening. He had no wish to linger over port with his future father-in-law, so the entire party moved back to the drawing room at the end of the meal.

By ten o'clock, when the tea tray and coffee jug arrived, he was having difficulty keeping his eyes open. How the hell could he be so tired when for the past few days he'd done absolutely nothing? Then his valet was at the handles of his vehicle and he was

311

whisked away to a chorus of good nights.

Sampson was no longer coming every day but was due first thing tomorrow, which was fortuitous, as there was something most particular that he needed to discuss with him.

'I'm just next door as usual, my lord, and will come if you ring or call.'

'Thank you, Mason. Good night.'

⋆   ⋆   ⋆

When the doctor had visited the next morning, he was impatient to ask him some pertinent questions.

'I'm intending to be married in two weeks. Firstly, can I use crutches or must I remain in this? Secondly, I wish to be able to make love to my wife on our wedding night — is there any objection to that?'

The physician laughed. 'It would be better if you waited until June when you're able to walk normally but who am I to stand in the way of true love?

Do you have crutches made for you already?'

'I do — you can see them leaning against the wall on the far side of my bedchamber.'

The doctor vanished to inspect the items and returned with them under his arm. 'These will do perfectly, my lord. The break is healing faster than I'd expected. I think it will be in order for you to try these out next week.'

'And the other matter?'

'As long as nothing you do involves putting weight on your ankle then you'll do it no harm. I feel it behoves me to point out it might well be the future Lady Sawsbury who will be injured by your splints.'

'I can assure you that won't happen. There's no need for you to attend me again unless I send for you. Thank you for your expertise.'

The young man nodded and strolled out. The crutches were still within arm's reach and Simon was about to stretch out for them when his valet snatched them away.

'No, my lord. Not until the end of next week.'

'I wish you to take me outside; if you go through the drawing room and directly onto the terrace, I can foresee no problems with this contraption.'

The weather was warm for the first week of April and he tossed aside the rug which had been solicitously tucked around his lower limbs.

'Push me to the steps so I can see the park clearly. The wall blocks my vision everywhere else.'

'There are tables and chairs, sir; do you wish to set up one of them? You will have a better view and can work from there.'

Soon Simon was settled with his injured leg propped on a second chair. He had a pile of correspondence waiting to be attended to and he sent his valet to fetch it from the study. He'd never employed a secretary, as he much preferred to take care of as much business personally as he could. He had an excellent estate manager who was now a happy man as he had more than enough funds to set in motion the vital repairs and renewals for the farms and the workers' cottages.

An hour after his arrival, he saw two horses emerge from the woods at the far end of the park. His sister and his future wife were returning from their hack. They had promised to join him after their morning ride in order to finalise the arrangements for the treasure hunt. He rang the bell and instructed the footman to bring luncheon in an hour for the three of them.

\* \* \*

Bella patted Rufus on the neck as she dismounted. 'Good boy. The more I ride you, the better I like you. Silver Star goes well with you, Emily; are you satisfied with her?'

'Absolutely. She is as good as anything we have in our own stables. However, she is a trifle slow so I intend to find something speedier for the races.'

'We have half a dozen hunters and two of the carriage horses also go well under saddle. Unfortunately, none of them will tolerate a side-saddle.'

'Then I'll ride like you — I've got a similar divided skirt to yours and breeches to wear under them. Show me these hunters and I'll choose the one I like the best.'

*   *   *

Annie had hot water and a delightful confection in striped Indian cotton waiting for her. 'His lordship is on the terrace, miss, and sent his man to ask if you'll join him there.'

'Then I must hurry.'

Emily was emerging from her own apartment as she stepped out of her sitting room. 'We are to have luncheon *al fresco* with my brother.'

'My parents don't approve of picnics or eating in the fresh air so I'm certain they will not wish to join us.' She raised her hand and sniffed. 'I can still detect a whiff of the stables. I should have taken longer over my ablutions.'

'Too late to repine. I've not seen Aunt Jemima today. I wonder why she didn't come down to breakfast.'

'I'm sure she's not indisposed. I've never seen a healthier individual of any age, let alone someone in their sixties.'

When she stepped through the drawing room doors onto the terrace, she stopped so suddenly her friend walked into her and they all but fell head first.

'That was a spectacular entrance, girls. I take it you're impressed with the cold collation I've had set out for us.' Simon's welcoming smile almost caused her to stumble a second time.

'It looks quite delicious and far too much for the three of us,' Emily said.

The three of them enjoyed every morsel of the meal and whilst eating, they finalised the plans for the treasure hunt.

'The doctor's given me permission to use my crutches from next week so I'll be able to walk, albeit slowly, down the aisle when we get married. I can't tell you how sorry I am that we won't be able to take a wedding trip as planned.'

'We've got the rest of our lives to explore the country together. Do you know when you will be able to travel? We have to be out of this house at the end of next month . . . '

'I'm hoping to be walking normally by then, so I'm certain we can depart for Sawsbury immediately after our nuptials. Once I'm able to hobble about the place without assistance then I can see no reason to delay.'

'I would feel guilty abandoning my parents when they'll have so much packing and organising to do.'

Mrs Featherstone marched out to join them and overheard this last remark. 'Good gracious, once the knot is tied you will be answerable to your husband and not to your father. I've agreed to remain here and assist with their removal. I cannot tell you how much I'm looking forward to the prospect of being useful once more.'

Mama and Aunt Jemima were obviously now on the way to becoming bosom bows, which would be excellent for both ladies.

'It's becoming chilly out here, my boy, I think you should be inside.' Without asking his permission, she picked up the brass bell and rang it. When a footman appeared again, she spoke for Simon.

'Kindly wheel his lordship back to his quarters.' She gestured towards the doors. 'Come along, girls, I'm sure there are plenty of tasks you can occupy yourself with until dinner time.'

Bella was about to protest but glanced at him and saw he was looking tight-lipped and pale. How could she have missed this and allowed someone else to step in?

Emily nodded and the three of them walked off, leaving him to transfer himself from the chair to his vehicle. She was remiss in her duties and was determined to do better in future.

★ ★ ★

The next week she was so busy helping her mother decide which items of furniture, which ornaments and which pictures she wished to take with her to the much smaller house that she scarcely had time to think about the way her life was going to change in a little over a sennight.

The weather continued to improve and she was beginning to get excited about the house party. The day before the first of the guests were expected to arrive, she was on the terrace with Simon.

'You will be pleased to know I've inspected all the punts and they are sound.'

He smiled lazily. 'I don't give a fig about them. Do you intend to go in one?'

'I dislike swimming or boats — so no, I don't.'

'In which case there's no need to discuss it further. I would enjoy this so much more if I could participate myself. I'm going to find it damnably difficult sitting on the sidelines like this whilst you flit about with handsome officers at your heels.'

'I do hope you're not going to be a jealous husband, my lord, and frown and fret whilst I'm dancing.' Her response had been light-hearted, and she turned, expecting him to be laughing with her.

Instead, his eyes were sad and for a second he looked like a stranger.

# 17

By late afternoon, all the guests were safely settled in their chambers, and for the first time in the three years that she'd lived there, Bella actually approved of Hawksford. The huge house looked different with the plethora of hothouse flower arrangements everywhere. It also sounded alive and exciting as there was a constant murmur of voices and a clatter of feet as the fifty or so guests, plus their personal servants, made themselves comfortable.

There'd been no time to spend alone with Simon as she'd been constantly in and out of the main hall greeting the next arrivals. Lord and Lady Danbury and their silly daughters had been tardy and had only just ascended to their apartment on the family side of the house.

'Well, I can't tell you how pleased I am that this wretched place has finally been of some use to us,' her mother said.

'I'm sure that Simon and I will entertain on a grand scale once we're married and you will be able to join in without having all the fuss to worry about.'

'Your papa has employed a musical trio for the duration of the house party. Two to play violins and the other the piano. He insists there will be dancing tonight and every night. I've never seen him so jubilant.'

'Is the thought of my marrying an aristocrat so pleasing to him?'

'No, I think that finding his fleet was not lost entirely is what's making him so happy. Also, he finally admitted that he disliked this house as much as we do and is eager to live somewhere more comfortable.'

'I just checked the dining room. I'd no idea the central table pulled out to seat so many. It will be a sad crush having everyone around it but better than a dozen or so sitting in the breakfast parlour.'

'We cannot linger here, Bella. We must retire to our rooms and begin our preparations for the evening. Champagne is to be served in the drawing room at five o'clock so please make sure you arrive before that.'

Her mother, despite her advancing years, was surprisingly light on her feet and ran up the staircase beside her. Annie had put out the evening gown that she'd chosen from the dozen she had in her closet.

As she had bathed two days ago, there was no need to repeat the process and a quick wash was all that was necessary. She sat in her underpinnings whilst her maid dressed her hair. Tonight, she was wearing a parure of diamonds and emeralds that Papa had had made especially for her on one of his trips to India.

It was almost a quarter to five o'clock before she was ready to leave her room. Her silk evening ensemble consisted of a pale green underskirt and silver net overskirt. Her evening slippers and gloves were emerald silk to match her jewellery.

'There, miss; you look like a princess. There'll be no other young lady as beautiful as you.'

Bella viewed herself from all sides in the long glass and was forced to admit she'd never looked better. The emeralds in her tiara sparkled against her russet hair, the necklace, ear-bobs and her emerald betrothal ring completed the picture.

If only her beloved could walk in beside her then everything would be perfect. In this ensemble, hurrying was not advisable as the material was flimsy and the slightest tug might tear it. 'I just heard Lady Emily come out of her apartment. I'll go down with her.'

Her future sister looked quite spectacular. 'I'm so glad you have also ignored the rule for debutantes and have worn colour. Gold and buttercup yellow are perfect with your dark colouring.'

They linked arms and made their careful way along the passage and down the staircase. She hoped Simon would be waiting for her in his chair, but the only occupants of the hall were three of the officers — she misremembered their names, but two were captains and one a major — and all the handsome young men looked magnificent in their finest regimentals.

The hand resting on her arm tightened. She glanced across at Emily and saw her friend was paying particular attention to the major. Was this how the land lay? Had Mrs Featherstone's acquaintances been included so that this particular officer could be present?

The major saw them coming and marched, parade-ground stiff, to the foot of the staircase. The other two followed suit.

Bella curtsied and Emily did the same. The officers introduced themselves again and after much bowing and fussing they were escorted into the drawing room. After her initial reservations about being paid so much attention, she began to relax and enjoy herself, and quite forgot that she should have been waiting for her betrothed, and not flirting with handsome officers, however harmless this might be.

★  ★  ★

Simon had been practising swinging around his apartment on his crutches for the past two days and was confident he would be able to maintain his balance and his dignity for the entire evening. He couldn't wait to see the face of his beloved girl when she saw him upright.

It had taken slightly longer than he'd anticipated to adjust his adapted evening trousers and to be certain he looked the best he could in the circumstances.

'Remain near enough for me to call you if I need your assistance tonight, Mason.'

'Yes, my lord.'

Fortunately, the distance from his ground floor apartment to the main reception rooms was not so far that he would be tired before he entered the drawing room. His intention had been to be in the hall as she approached but he realised most of the guests were already mingling. He would be unable to make his entrance as he'd hoped.

He paused in the doorway and from his height had the advantage of being able to see over the heads of most of the occupants. At first, he couldn't see her, but when one of the broad-shouldered officers moved aside, he saw her laughing up at him.

An emotion he didn't recognise surged through him, and he was about to barge his way across and make his displeasure clear to her and her admirers, when he reconsidered. God's teeth! He was jealous and that wasn't a pleasant thing to be. Why shouldn't Bella enjoy the evening and the admiration of the gentlemen surrounding her?

Then she looked across and saw him. Her expression changed and he knew in that moment that she reciprocated his feelings. Ignoring the officers, she gathered her skirts and ran towards him.

'Why didn't you tell me you could walk again? I should have preferred to come in with you. Those officers are quite tiresome, you know. My face aches from being obliged to smile at their nonsense.'

'Step into the hall with me. There's something I must say to you and should have told you two weeks ago.'

She didn't argue and they moved away from the doorway so they could not be seen by those inside the chamber.

'There's something I must tell you too. Shall you go first, or will I?'

He braced his shoulder against the panelling and drew her close. 'I love you, my darling, and have done so since the moment I set eyes on you.'

Her squeal of joy brought several curious guests from the drawing room. He ignored them all.

'I love you too. I can't tell you when it happened but I realised last week and didn't know if I should tell you.'

He tightened his grip and she came willingly. Her soft curves were pressed against his chest. She tilted her face so he could kiss her.

A considerable time later he raised his head, too moved to speak. He reached up and straightened her tiara, which had come adrift during their passionate embrace.

'Darling, I hope you don't intend to flirt with those military gentlemen all evening.'

She stood on tiptoe and kissed him lightly. 'Even if I wished to, after the icy glare you gave them I doubt any of them would dare to come within two yards of me.'

'I was consumed by jealousy for a moment. I'm ashamed of myself for feeling thus, as I know you were only being polite.'

'My love, I cannot wait to be your wife and start my new life with you elsewhere.'

'I'm the luckiest man in Christendom to have found you.' He grinned and kissed the tip of her nose. 'I would have married you if you'd been penniless but your inheritance will make our lives so much easier.'

'And I would have married you if you were a commoner but being a countess will be rather splendid.'

In perfect harmony, they rejoined the company. He was well aware of the envious glances he received from not only the single gentlemen but the married ones as well.

They drifted into the dining room and he and Bella were seated at the head of the table, Burgoyne and his wife were to the left, and his sister and Mrs Featherstone on the right.

Champagne was poured and this time he was able to pick up his glass — doing so when balancing on his crutch was an impossibility. His future father-in-law stood up and the table fell silent.

'Thank you all for coming here and I hope you enjoy your stay. You will see in front of you an itinerary listing the events and activities that have been arranged for you all. Next weekend culminates in the most important occasion — the marriage of my only child to Lord Sawsbury.' He raised his glass and everyone at the table, apart from Bella and himself, stood up with their own glasses charged.

'To the future Earl and Countess of Sawsbury.'

★ ★ ★

The toast was drunk and there was not a soul sitting around that table who did not see at once that this was not an arranged marriage, as they had supposed, but a love match. Any of the guests who had harboured a lingering doubt about Miss Burgoyne's honour put it to one side. The earl and his future countess could start their married life with unblemished reputations. Everyone agreed they had never seen a happier couple.

THE RECLUSIVE DUKE
A LORD IN DISGUISE
CHRISTMAS AT DEVIL'S GATE
A MOST DELIGHTFUL CHRISTMAS
CHRISTMAS GHOSTS AT
THE PRIORY
A CHRISTMAS BETROTHAL
DUKE IN DANGER

We do hope that you have enjoyed reading this large print book.

Did you know that all of our titles are available for purchase?

We publish a wide range of high quality large print books including:
**Romances, Mysteries, Classics**
**General Fiction**
**Non Fiction and Westerns**

Special interest titles available in large print are:
**The Little Oxford Dictionary**
**Music Book, Song Book**
**Hymn Book, Service Book**

Also available from us courtesy of Oxford University Press:
**Young Readers' Dictionary**
**(large print edition)**
**Young Readers' Thesaurus**
**(large print edition)**

For further information or a free brochure, please contact us at:
**Ulverscroft Large Print Books Ltd.,**
**The Green, Bradgate Road, Anstey,**
**Leicester, LE7 7FU, England.**
**Tel:** (00 44) **0116 236 4325**
**Fax:** (00 44) **0116 234 0205**

# LOVING LADY SARAH

## J. Darley

As life returns to normal after the war, Lady Sarah Trenton's reality is put into perspective. Her love for Robert, the gamekeeper's son who has returned home safely, is as alive as ever. But they must meet in secret, for Lord Trenton, whose heart has been hardened by the loss of his son, intends to see his daughter marry a man of wealth and status — like the odious Sir Percy. The times are changing, but the class divide is as wide as ever. Will Sarah and Robert be forced apart?

# FORBIDDEN FLOWERS

## Alice Elliott

An embarrassing slip in the Hyde Park mud leads Lily and Rose Banister into the path of Philip Montgomery, a British Embassy diplomat. Mesmerised by Lily's beauty, he invites her to accompany him to the Paris Exhibition, while Rose, who can't help but feel envious, is asked to chaperone the trip. Arriving in Paris, the trio happen upon Philip's old adversary Gordon Pomfret, who decides to join their group, obviously vying for Lily's attention. Meanwhile, Rose and Philip discover that their shared interests might just make them kindred spirits . . .